RUBY'S
Covert
MISSION

"If you are heading back to Hobart on an autumn day,

You will see the mountain rising over Sandy Bay.

When you feel that light wind blowing up from old Iron Pot,

Then, you know you are surely blessed with what you've got.

Come and roam our island home

And always have a place to call your own.

Hear the wind call you home

It is time. Return with sails aloft, full blown.

Have you heard the cat play fiddle in the city mall

Or have you shopped in Salamanca at a market stall

Or explored the Channel sailing out from Oyster Cove?

Oh, there's always somewhere close, to rest or rove.

Come and roam, fresh air and crashing foam,

See the rolling hills and rivers roam.

Hear the wind call you home

It is time. Return with sails aloft, full blown."

(Words and Music by Stefan Nicholson)

Other relevant books by Stefan A. Nicholson

'SAN Language Book of Instruction'

'Business Analysis Package'

'Peripheral Lives'

'Blind Familiarity'

'Symbolic Art Notation'

'JEMMA short stories'

'CIRCLE in a SPIRAL'

'SPY within a RUBY'

'DIAMOND for a RUBY'

'Shadows, Anxiety & Narrative'

"Quick Stories for Quick Kids'

SV "Nickinoff" - Hobart

There is also a music CD – 'Pictures of Life'

"For she shines like the moon, that fairest maiden sublime, showing such an air and deportment that gives her away. With an image that steers my thoughts throughout each meandering day . . . before such feelings overwhelm my idle soul's affray"

– Stefan Nicholson

RUBY'S Covert MISSION   First Edition June 2019

Copyright © 2019 Stefan Andrew Nicholson, Hobart Tasmania

All rights reserved   Printed Book

Printed in Australia

ISBN: 978-0-6482953-5-8

Published by:

ENVIROSUPPORT

P.O. Box 370, South Hobart,

Tasmania, Australia 7004

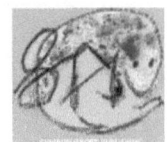

Website: www.stefannicholson.com

email: stefannicholson@bigpond.com

phone: +61 417 181 077

CONTENTS

Ruby Returns

R uby emerged bedraggled from the coach wearing her favourite black beret, perched sideways over her neatly gathered hair. It looked decidedly odd. After stretching and arching her back, she let out a huge drawn-out yawn with a sound that surprised her.

The driver had difficulty containing his amusement as Ruby attempted to throw a thick tangerine-and-white football scarf around her neck. She pretended not to notice him, whilst nervously checking out her appearance in the door window, squinting at her reflection, homing in on the huge 'Kiss-Me-Quick' strap-bag by her side – an impulse buy from the souvenir shop in Blackpool. Raising her eyebrows lazily, she wondered why she had brought it back to London, an immediate give-away, as to where she had been. It was such a silly mistake, she thought, shaking her head and looking over towards the distant taxi rank.

Ruby again felt the secretive glances of the driver, following her around like a hesitant parent on their child's first day at school. She turned and smiled at him kindly. Looking rather embarrassed, he smiled back awkwardly, unable to take his eyes off her, as he pretended to do his paperwork, his eyes drifting back to this tall willowy young woman with the haunted eyes and such an apparent inner sadness, now looking up and down the road for any sign of a taxi or Metro-Bus.

Ruby cut a lonely figure against the softened distant sandstone buildings as rain-speckled windows reflected the moonlight from her face - the orange glow from street lamps, intermittently illuminating her body through the swaying appendages of trees.

Ruby contemplated the consequences of her secret expedition to Blackpool, having recovered Roger's private papers from a safe-deposit box at the bus station. It had revealed a vast wealth, quietly accumulated over his lifetime, skilfully embedded within secret bank accounts, false identities and private property.

It was all legally prepared as expected, albeit using several fake names but everything was accessible without raising any alarms.

It now belonged to her, if she could only take leave from her new work duties to make her way to Australia to claim it.

Staring out into the mist, thinking about what Roger would have said to her about her present circumstances, she knew that he would have had none of her sentimentality. He often warned her to be careful of burying emotional connections to past events, saying it was the weakest link in an agent's limited mental armoury – just waiting to surface unexpectedly, in moments of pity, love, sadness or hate. Ruby had experienced all that and more . . . she had lost her Eric. She missed his nerdy ways and uncanny random logic, which always mystified her. She missed his love and affection and caring.

Having had time for reflection since Roger Davis had died, murdered by a British elite terrorist group three years ago, she had now become a graduate Field Information Officer (FIO) Grade 3, with MI6.

Her friend and mentor, the ex-Chinese agent Tian, recruited by Davis as a double agent, said that it would help her to understand her place in the world if she could just finish what she had started, before allowing time to grieve for her lost love . . . before moving on. Tian knew that Ruby's love for Eric Johnson was like her own passion for Ilya Kasparov. Both had died at the hands of brutal forces from the darker side of life, where the devil within the human psyche acts like a cruel leveller to innocence and hope.

The same sociopath who had butchered Eric had also tricked Ruby into meeting with him in a church, where he attacked her mercilessly, pinning her down in the confessional box. It was only Tian's quick thinking and unwavering dedication to duty that saved Ruby from an evil, horrendous death. Firing two bullets into the head of Feliks at any other time would always have been an act of kindness, releasing his mind from what he had witnessed and had twisted into a frenzied hatred for MI6.

Eric once occupied Ruby's every waking moment, affecting her thinking and willingness to survive, prompting Tian to warn her that the time to grieve had passed, or else she would always be angry, wanting justice, revenge . . . maybe even an 'escape' from herself.

"Be strong Ruby. Life's journey is sometimes so sad . . . so perhaps you should take another road, in order to make the right choice," she would whisper, each time Ruby relapsed into sadness.

At school, Ruby had hated life and everyone in it. Her height and strength had been no match for the bullies, but loneliness had become her friend, until Eric had come to her rescue, by chance. He had always loved her from a distance but lacked the courage to approach her, half-expecting to be the recipient of the 'shin-kick', which she used frequently, to repel unwanted intruders. Ruby's awkward expression often displayed her uneasy life to others, enough for them to be wary of her. She was still questioning everything, including her natural beauty and emotions.

Ruby remembered 'that slip of paper' given to her by a teacher, who had sought to ease her worries. Ruby knew the real reason . . . that he had strong feelings for her. She in turn wanted someone to care about her . . . and liked the innocent amorous attention.

She could still recite the words:

"Life is not a rigid road to follow dutifully at the whim of others who seek to control the wild spirit within you. Keep your distance from their dull limitations on how people should live, for they are unaware that they are only slaves to fashionable normality. You must rise above their failings to reveal to the world . . . the person you really are."

When she had quoted the note slowly to Eric, he had listened quietly, expressionless, before reaching out to hold her, whispering his brief reply, whilst kissing her neck lightly.

"My philosophy on life is simple . . . I don't have one. I have you in my life. That's all I want. I can write you a fancy note too . . . if you like."

It was Davis the 'undercover tradesman', who had thrown the two of them together unexpectedly, by allowing them to be a small part of his MI6 surveillance team at the age of sixteen. That small part developed into a tragic mistake, as it escalated rapidly into a series of ever-increasing dangererous consequences.

Ruby turned away from the bus driver to wipe away an inopportune tear, realising that it only takes a single moment to relive such moments. A noisy car sped past, breaking her train of thought - splashing icy water onto her bare legs. She did not hear what obscenities they were shouting and did not much care.

The bus driver shook his head with disapproval before checking his watch. It was getting late. The riff raff were making their noisy way home. Ruby wanted to go home too, to a hot shower and her nice warm bed.

She wondered what MI6 would be thinking about her absence. They had rattled her confidence in them, just before her trip, bugging her unit and maintaining surveillance from a white van across the street. It was no way to win her over to their questionable ethics, she thought.

Tian had now become her supervisor, balancing a fine line between continuing her covert surveillance of Ruby and being her close friend. However, she had become suffocatingly close, always checking up on her movements and asking about her private life. Ruby suspected that Tian was monitoring her movements and state of mind, because of 'C's annoyance with her attitude.

The 'company' wanted to know if Ruby knew anything more about Davis and his stash of personal papers. They presumed he had hidden them carefully. They wanted to know if they contained any damaging consequences. In fact, many people wanted those papers – badly, with some believing that he had stumbled across the key to an old threat, that could come back to haunt them.

It was rumoured to be about a global threat, involving weapons of mass destruction (WMDs). Davis being a perfectionist was forced into keeping it secret, as he trusted nobody and was well aware that MI6 was under a cloud. It was widely known at that time, that a 'mole' had infiltrated the organisation at a senior level.

Ruby refocussed on getting home. It had to be a cash transaction of course, to hide her whereabouts from any digital audit trail. However, there were still no taxis on the rank and she was now getting rather anxious about carrying so much cash on her.

The bus driver kept looking at her with sideway glances. Ruby guessed that he was waiting to see if anyone was coming to pick her up or if she required a taxi. It was a Saturday night after all, when taxis are hard to find. She had left her phone and credit cards at home too, because they were such easy markers for anyone wanting to track her movements.

The driver finally caught her gaze and looked at her nervously, trying to find a speedy solution. Then he whispered a few words into his phone, before fully winding down the window.

"Can I call a taxi for you love or are you waiting for someone?" he shouted out over the noise of some passing traffic.

Ruby looked relieved, that someone actually cared about her.

"I thought that the taxi rank would have at least one car waiting, being next to a bus depot. Can you recommend another taxi rank nearby? I want to pay with cash - otherwise I would have ordered an Uber . . . but I left my phone and cards at home."

The driver waived his hand and pointed to a taxi that was slowly trawling down the road. It was obvious that the cabbie did not know whether to stop or not. It looked like a contrived situation.

"There you are then lass. Your thoughts have been answered."

Ruby smiled back at him briefly, noticing a secret connection between him and the taxi driver. She waved down the taxi anyway, turning back towards the bus.

"Thank you for a most relaxing ride. Good night . . . and thank you for waiting."

The driver looked in awe at her silhouetted profile against the taxi headlights. Her pale face shone like the moon's glow over an icy lake . . . indeed appearing 'beyond words', as Roger Davis had told him many years ago.

"I'll let Jacko know that you arrived safely and are on your way home. He told me to look after you . . . to make sure you were safe. He hopes to see you again. We all do. Good night love, and take care."

It had started raining heavily as the taxi driver raced around to the front passenger door to open it, whilst giving her a friendly smile. He then looked up at the bus driver and gave him a discreet nod. Ruby was in safe hands and the bus driver could finally make his phone call to let Jacko know that Ruby was on her way home.

"Red Gem has been assigned to the 'next shift', over."

"I read you Transporter. Return to 'rock capital', over."

Davis would have sighed, then shaken his head in disbelief at all the unnecessary symbolism. He would then have surely expected the wry smiles from this band of outcasts to follow . . . his most trusted colleagues . . . his only true friends.

"Hello Miss . . . and where can I take you this evening?" asked the cabbie cautiously on seeing her introspective outlook.

Ruby was again preoccupied with her thoughts but this time about getting into her apartment. She managed a faint smile back, which pleased the driver enough to encourage his eager banter.

"The drizzly rain can be a bit off-putting when arriving in London on a weekend. So, where are you going then? I see that you've been up North for a spell. I love the beaches, the piers and that Golden Mile. Now when I was a lad . . . ."

"I wonder . . . if you can drop me off . . . behind the Redmond Place building. Do you know it? I need to go to the back entrance."

"I certainly do Miss. That is a grand building. Be there in ten minutes . . . and I'll wait with my lights on until you're safely inside."

"Oh no, that's not necessary. I . . . I have to actually jump over the back wall . . . as I . . . I forgot my gate key again," replied Ruby hesitantly, screwing up her nose.

"Doing a bit of 'moonlighting', eh? That's not a problem love. Well, not for you anyway. You are obviously much fitter than I am . . . and younger . . . and lighter. Although you may need to wear some leather gloves I would think, to scale a rough wall. And with your bare legs and all . . ."

Ruby looked rather embarrassed but managed to placate him.

"It's all above board, really . . . and I should probably not have told you. You can drop me down the road from there, if you prefer."

"Oh that's alright, I've been in much worse situations than that Ruby . . . I've had quite some time in the security services you know. Well . . . you can see just how successful that was," he replied with a laugh and then a frown.

Ruby had not mentioned her name. That meant he could be MI6 or more likely, one of Jacko's cronies. He looked friendly enough and not agency-indented - but then most spies do have that outgoing capacity to engage with their 'victims'. Then there was the secret interaction with the bus driver.

"Please give my regards to Jacko then. I'm sure he will be quite amused at how my trip ended, what with my disappearing over the back wall at Redmond Place," she said slowly with a faint smile.

"Ah, yes, right you are then. I know I slipped up there . . . what with your name and all, didn't I? Just don't tell Jacko that I'm an absolute idiot, ok?"

Ruby laughed, "Absolutely . . . not. I will not say anything to anybody as long as you tell me your name . . . your real name that is. I've had rather enough of the enthusiastic nicknames that people choose for themselves."

"Just call me 'Shifter'. Well, that is what everyone calls me. I get things done right, the first time and move people and other assets around in a safe and secure way."

"I would be worried if you were called 'Cleaner' with a contract on me or even 'Shifty' for that matter. So what was the deal with Davis and Jacko then? I mean, to me it looks like you were all working together as a sort of 'band of brethren' . . . and knowing Roger, he would never choose just anybody. But I won't put you on the spot . . . if you don't want to say anything more, Shifter."

Shifter looked at her, sitting there looking at him like a wide-eyed puppy, weighing up what little he knew about her with what he could not possibly know, being out of the 'company' for some time.

"Well, yes, that would be a fair description I suppose. We all have the expert skills and international contacts to do what you will be doing. The main difference is that we do it within the spirit of a closed group of friends. We share the same feelings and expectations to obtain the results we want to achieve. We help those who can't help themselves to get a fair outcome to their problems. There are some very nasty individuals out there."

"Blimey, it sounds very Robin Hood. But why did Roger or the rest of you want to operate under the radar?"

"There is no trickery or politics in how we operate Ruby, unlike MI6 having to act within the rules of crown, law and diplomacy. Then there were those damn 'moles' that seem to surface on a regular basis, to protect . . . well let's just say . . . the elevated interests of others."

Ruby knew that MI6 'moles' had betrayed Davis, leading to the horrendous death of Kata Bielski and the torture of her son Feliks, who went on to butcher her Eric in the wine cellar of the Mayfair Mews Hotel in Dogbol.

The gruesome experiences endured by Feliks at the hands of the Russians had driven him to insanity. He had become a sociopath with a nasty way of displaying his handiwork . . . mercilessly cutting his victim to pieces, scattering dismembered body parts around the scene of his crimes. Then there was his chilling calling card – a sharp object, a pen, a stick or a knife - thrust into the victim's eye.

Ruby began to feel anxious again. She took a few deep breaths, before forcing herself to think about how she was going to enter her apartment. Shifter looked away, still rambling on about his days in the 'company' and how he had prepared various papers for his 'people' – which Ruby didn't understand at first.

Ruby was a quiet audience for the remainder of the trip, skilfully charmed by this enthusiastic lecturer into relaxing a little. The ride was highly enlightening as she smiled now and again in between closing her eyes. She now knew more about 'forging passports' than she would ever need to know.

At one point, she removed the passports from her bag that Roger had given to her . . . and wondered. As he was driving, Shifter looked at her occasionally. When he saw the passports that Davis had organised for Ruby and Eric, he started laughing to himself.

"Now there's a fine work of artistic license, for sure," he whispered.

Sure enough, it was Shifter who had produced them, although 'Scarlett Angel' still seemed a bit colourful, even though she had been 'reinvented' as an actor, of all things. She had a quiet giggle about what Davis would have been thinking, which made Shifter laugh along with her. Then she looked at Eric's passport, with the name 'Damon Spier', the new alias for Eric 'Diamond' Johnson – an identity that would now never exist.

Shifter kept looking at her, admiring the beauty of her face and the wayward strands of hair gliding over her cheek . . . she seemed so incredibly interesting and unfathomable, occasionally offering a brief smile before withdrawing into her thoughts once more.

He could feel her pain, having lived through the same trauma of losing friends and colleagues. He reflected that such a turbulent life is not one that should be lived by a person who has feelings - especially by someone so young.

Ruby started to read Roger's letter again . . . his final words. She always felt that he was somehow close by, still looking after her in some unfathomable way. Then she thought about the luscious vanilla slice and that creamy coffee with the smiley face, served at the cafe in Stanley Park. The waitress had also given her some friendly advice:

"A friend is both hard to find and even harder to lose my dear. Do not waste too much time over past relationships. Life is too short to be living in the past love."

She felt a lump in her throat as she remembered Eric fronting up to her house, swelled up by his newly found importance as the undercover 'Diamond' – recruited so young by Davis.

"Ruby . . . Ruby I want to ask you if you will have dinner with me tonight at the restaurant . . . and . . . and I will not take no for an answer," he had blurted out.

It was supposed to have been such a simple observation exercise: times, people, car registrations . . . but a reality that turned into a downward spiral of misery and death.

Her present emotions and reflections were certainly inconsistent with visiting Blackpool for the weekend. She imagined that most young women of her age would be thinking of love, fashion, and enjoying life – trying to meet someone special to share their love. However, Ruby was not average, nor normal and not tied to the fashionable stereotypes of how most people live their lives.

She tensed up and took a deep breath. It was already 9-50pm and she still had to break into her own home, without being seen. Not that she would be in any actual trouble, but Ruby did not want her work colleagues to know that she had 'skipped off' for a day.

Analysing the situation at hand, Ruby visualised the glass-spiked wall she would have to scale, before dropping eight feet into the garbage area and its horrible smells. Her leather waistcoat would serve as a barrier to the broken glass surface. She was hoping too, that the rubbish had been collected - especially the mountain of putrid seafood remnants from apartment 23. The wrapping paper once showed the apartment number, but strangely enough, Ruby had never seen the people who lived there, quiet, unseen and mysterious. With the amount of seafood waste neatly wrapped up in butcher's paper, she mused that maybe an old woman with twenty cats lived there. The fishy smell sometimes extended outside of the apartment . . . and into the corridor near her apartment.

Ruby decided to use a trick way of accessing the lift and door-entry pads to her apartment, having already secretly tested it. She had created a fake electronic entry key, using Eric's electronic scanner-reader-writer, to match the identity of a temporarily vacant apartment, on the same floor.

The main aim with this approach was to make sure that the security cameras did not register her face as she was pushing the buttons on her key pad. A quick squirt of Eric's 'smother cream' would fix that.

It was a black fluid, which turned into a dark ice when sprayed onto a glass surface – enough to cover the camera lens. When the ice melted, the black specks would wash away with the fluid, leaving little trace. Ruby was all set for her 'break-in'.

The taxi stopped in the dark lane just behind the Redmond Place apartments. It was cold but at least the rain had stopped. Ruby put on her gloves and placed the strap-bag behind her like a rucksack. She opened the door, hesitated and turned back with a smile.

> "Thank you Shifter, I do hope we meet again to talk more about what you do. It is nice to know that others share my philosophy on life. You are very thoughtful and caring – all of you."

> "Take care Ruby. You are highly skilled with a great empathy for others. You know where you can find us if need be. We are always available to render assistance . . . anywhere, anytime," replied Shifter, touching her arm before she disappeared into the night.

Ruby waited near the perimeter wall until the taxi had disappeared into the night. Using her steel-fibre reinforced, leather belt she scaled the wall with ease, waiting for a few seconds perched on top of her waist coast, before dropping down to the ground.

A firm hand grabbed her shoulder blade forcibly, scaring her, immobilising her, causing her to panic - until she turned around.

> "Well, well. The covert agent has returned from her magical mystery tour . . . and assumed she was all alone. I taught you to be vigilant at all times."

> "Tian! . . . What the hell are you doing here frightening me like that? Is it a crime for an agent to practice her craft? Anyway, I went on a trip in my own time, to get away from you all. Is that a crime too? And what about you, sneaking around my apartment building in the middle of the night . . . on a weekend . . . in my time off," barked Ruby.

Tian looked at her, realising that her orders to follow Ruby, in the hope that she might lead her to the Davis' papers was a flawed move. They had formed a close bond until now. However, as it was highly reasonable to expect that Ruby was the only one trusted to sort out Davis's financial and personal matters on his death . . . Tian understood why she had orders to retrieve them - at all costs.

"You can't keep following my every move Tian. I do have a private life too you know. I just wanted to see if I could escape the gaze of the 'company', knowing full well, that they would be trying to follow me. I am not the enemy . . . I am one of you."

Tian looked uncomfortable, the brushed it aside. Nothing would ever prevent her from completing a mission.

"I was only trying to protect you . . . again. You may remember that I have saved your life on numerous occasions 'Miss Scarlett O'Really', because of your lack of training and limited experience in the field," shouted Tian.

Ruby sighed and calmed down to avoid making a scene.

"Yes, alright, alright, I appreciate your concerns but at the same time, I knew that you would be following me in the hope that I would lead you to Rogers' private papers - if he ever had any. I certainly have not found any and if you remember, I graduated with a Grade Three and that makes me capable of looking after myself from now on."

Tian looked at her quizzically for any subtle clues. Ruby did not have any bags, or envelopes . . . or anything.

"Travelling light then for a full day away Ruby? There is a whole day of blanks to fill in . . . and you have nothing with you at all. Not even a handbag or purse . . . nothing at all."

Then Tian noticed that Ruby was not wearing any of her favourite clothing, shoes or hat, that she had bugged. Ruby gave her a grin as she removed her beret, which contained Eric's spray bottle, shaking her long hair and taking a slow deep breath.

"And you'll never know where I have been or what I did . . . because I beat you at your own game. I was formless and I liked it. I mean, it was in my own time, my weekend and my life. You have no right to shadow me . . . but thank you for your concern. I may have to follow you, one of these days."

Tian looked away in thought, at the apartment building and then back to Ruby.

"So, how were you going to get back into your apartment then without being seen by the security guards, cameras or tripping all the electronic systems?"

Ruby pulled out her normal security key and dangled it in front of Tian. There was now no need to bypass anything.

"I'm not wanted for murder Tian. I was going to use my standard security device to enter the building, operate the lift and gain entry to my unit. Do you want to come up for a coffee, or are you going to frisk me before reporting back to 'C'," Ruby joked.

Tian was annoyed but presumed that Ruby had in fact just put her to the test for evading detection, in effect actually doing something that most new graduates would not have pulled off with such ease, if at all.

Tian smiled at Ruby and tapped her on the head.

"Well done Agent Peters. You have outwitted MI6 and now me. Unfortunately, I must go home and explain in my report to 'C', how I lost contact with you for twenty four hours."

"Will he be amused?" asked Ruby sheepishly.

"I think that he will be keeping a closer eye on you my girl and will probably hide the silver, if you ever have dinner with him."

Tian walked towards the front gate with a security device of her own, giving Ruby a weary wave. She had failed. Ruby expected that Tian had also been rummaging around in her apartment too, looking for any clues, papers, maybe some sensitive photos, plans or even weapons.

Ruby cautiously went back to the holding area near the garbage bins, carefully extracting her bag and contents from the wall, where she had made a gap between two layers of bricks.

"You'll have to do better than that 'C' if you want to get me to divulge what I know about Davis," she whispered to herself, screwing up her nose.

There was already a divergence between what MI6 did and what Ruby expected it to do. She had to agree that Davis had the right idea, by having a backup plan and working his two worlds together but separately. Yet, sadly he paid the ultimate price for his country.

On returning to her unit, she retrieved the 'MY6' badge that Davis had given her. She destroyed the serial number, located on the back plate - a coded location of the safety deposit box by post code, box number and PIN. Now there was no link between her and Jacko or to his 'Swiss Bus Company' in Blackpool.

The next item on her list was to scan for bugging devices using Eric's hand-made scanner. She discovered one device under her coffee table and one under her bed, removing them both, placing one in the lift with the continuous boring background music and one on the neighbour's white poodle. It had just ventured out into the corridor, ready for a last minute 'walk around the garden'.

"You sick bastards," she shouted out aloud into one of the devices.

Having left her phone, credit cards and drivers licence at home whilst she went on her trip, there was no audit trail of any of her movements over the weekend. She had also disposed of all her favourite clothing more than a week ago fearing they were bugged, and had bought new items the day before her trip, with cash. Cash is indeed king, she thought.

Looking at her bland choices, now all torn and stained from the rear-wall drop, she decided that a healthy shopping spree was in order. Her specialised training was starting to kick in and she was beginning to feel like a professional. All that she needed was a worthy cause to pursue within her job. Otherwise, she would have to find one of her own.

Unknown to Ruby, there was another part to the intrusive surveillance of her apartment. A white Ford Transit van, parked up the road from her unit had already sprung into life. With the engine started, two technicians sent to analyse the vibrations on her apartment windows and two listening devices, had packed up their surveillance gear. They had orders to go home, still recovering from Ruby's loud obscenities . . . and their meanings.

"Thank goodness we can have a night off for a change Reggie. She's a smart one, that one . . . and a real 'looker' too."

"Real nice that's for sure but too smart for our lot mate. She'll run rings around us will that one."

Back at Vauxhall Cross, 'C' was mulling over the sparse report from Tian and the news that the surveillance team sent to spy on Ruby had packed up early, again. This left Ruby without any coverage at all. He rubbed his chin before making a quick phone call.

"Simon, do we still have that meeting with the CIA and ASIS at Pine Gap next month? Well, there is another team member I would like over there. Yes, Ruby Peters will be joining you. I want her well away from here, for a while and I've been advised quite heatedly, that the CIA would like to talk with her about what happened in Liverpool with some of their rogue agents, some years ago . . . and most likely about the loss of those bloody diamonds again."

His eyes narrowed as he read the final words of Tian's report.

"Ruby needs to be given something worthwhile to do! We cannot afford to lose her. We owe her a new start after what she has been through."

Giving operational advice to 'C' was never a good idea at the best of times and now was a particularly bad time. The whereabouts of Davis's stash and the state of his mind just before his death, in relation to his work with MI6 was unknown. There was a rumour that he could have been 'compromised'. Maybe he had been 'turned' like the others. Ruby was the only person who could ever answer those questions. However, whether she would ever tell anybody, was what had many people worried – and they would have to pursue her relentlessly for any information concerning Davis.

The fact that Ruby appeared to doubt the integrity of the 'company' was another worry, as she had good reason, given the circumstances of her turbulent association with Davis. It did not help their cause by tagging her and following her about with all their resources.

All for One

Ruby woke up at 5am on the Monday morning. After only four hours of meaningful sleep on the Saturday night, she had gone to bed at 10pm on Sunday after a quiet day of listening to her classical music.

It was during this idle time that she realised her perception of MI6, and particularly Tian and 'C' was being influenced by her inability to let go of her demons. Davis had not given up on them, quite the contrary. He died in active service, protecting not only Ruby and her family, but also the safety of the British Government and its people. She wanted to be just like him. His mistake of hiring her as a minor had fortuitously given her that opportunity. He had now also given her the means to escape.

Ruby identified the existence of the 'moles' as the real weakness in the 'company', which had made her feel unsafe at the time, but they had now all been exposed and dealt with.

She was feeling rather smug at the prospect of starting her internship with 'C' himself, after finding some of the information he had formally requested at her graduation ceremony. She decided it was time to pacify his concerns by being the best agent she could be - and to give it her all.

On her way down in the lift to the car park, Ruby looked up at the speaker. She remembered the bugging device, originally planted in her room was still where she had relocated it. She pitied the technician listening to the endless recorded music, those insipid pieces of bland synthesiser 'mixes', all day and all night. She expected the surveillance vehicle to be nearby.

Approaching her car affectionately nicknamed Max from the 'Ruby and Max' TV show, Ruby was prepared to see just how far they would go. She had brought Eric's scanner with her.

'Beep, Beep, Beep,' sounded the alarm . . . in two locations. One was sandwiched into a groove, cut into the upholstery of the passenger-side sun visor. The other was located under the roof rack bar, to record the outside sounds.

Ruby carefully picked them out and placed them underneath the main-gate drive motor – guaranteed to make a lot of noise every time the gate opened . . . and closed. Of course, this action was not going to win many friends at the field operations office, but it did show that she was up to the challenge of looking after herself.

The two weary men in the white van across the road, ordered to get back on the job, stared at her car as she drove past . . . waving wildly at them, with a wide grin. They started packing up again, even before contacting their supervisor, each sharing a secret admiration for the 'up yours' attitude that Ruby was showing to the establishment. It also allowed them to go home early again, stopping off at the drive-through for some 'bacon and egg muffins' and chai lattes.

Ruby was now in 'spy mode', knowing that placing two men in a van would not be the only surveillance strategy used to monitor her.

As she travelled to work, she quickly noticed a black Audi following behind her, interchanged with a silver Mercedes and then a white Astra at various points along her route. Ruby picked out the first two vehicles at once, for it seemed to her that they were a bit too controlled in their movements and stayed too far back.

However, she really was no longer concerned about surveillance tactics, turning up the radio. She had decided to stop playing silly games with them. After all, she was one of 'them' now and needed to show some sensibility . . . and respect.

In the car park area, the white Astra pulled up fast behind her. The darkened window wound down. It was Tian. From the calm look on her face, it seemed that their little misunderstanding over the weekend was now over.

> "Good morning Ruby. Your first day in a new job and I want to tell you that . . . yes, you are entitled to have your own private time. So, why don't we start off on a new level playing field. We are still good friends and now we are also professional colleagues at work."

> "Good morning Tian. Sounds fair to me. Thank you for understanding that. So, when does the surveillance stop? I am

sure there are better ways of spending the resources of the 'company'."

Tian smiled at her and parked her car. They both walked to the security entrance together where each presented their pass credentials – electronic tag, retina and fingerprint recognition. Tian waved her arm towards one of the long corridors leading to downward steps.

"Come, I will take you to our office. It is a bit of a walk but well worth it. 'C' usually spends a few minutes with us unless there is an issue somewhere else, and we never know when of course. Habits are frowned upon here. They lead to coincidence, which leads to vulnerability and . . ."

"I can't help thinking that our entrance to the building was so . . . easy," interrupted Ruby gingerly.

Tian raised her eyebrows and nodded approvingly.

"The entrance has facial-recognition for matching biometrics, temperature and salinity level on your face. Your fingerprint is decoded for DNA, presence of drugs and common poisons, explosives . . . your body is weighed . . . there is a metal detector and body scanner and . . . well, I for one know who you are young lady."

Ruby was impressed and Tian was pleasantly surprised at Ruby's need for assurance.

"A good agent never takes anything for granted. A great agent thinks outside of the box. Roger told me that, when I first worked with him outside of the 'company'. He was the only person I would ever trust with my life. We went through hell on that assignment, but he always remained calm, truthful and above all, honest."

"So, you knew him well? I mean . . . with him being so alone with his thoughts and personal life," asked Ruby casually.

"I worked with him over eight years on Interpol–related matters and yet I can guess that you knew him far better than I did. We were both formally recruited at the same time, as was Ilya but in different countries. We had already developed our self-awareness through the field experience that you never had. I think Roger saw you as someone to nourish and protect. You know, he made a serious error getting you and Eric involved in his surveillance . . . sixteen indeed. However, I am glad you are with us now. Your experiences have not all been bad you know. I do not know anyone else like you, to have survived such ordeals as you have. But now you must put everything else aside, to concentrate on your job and your allegiance to your country."

Ruby was unsure why Tian had told her these things.

"I was thinking about my past attitude and future with the 'company' over the weekend, and you know what, I've been rather silly in blaming everything on them. Just one thing bothers me Tian. How do I cope with doing something that I really do not want to do? What if I find something very unethical about my orders and get sent to some foreign country with the orders . . . say, to kill someone I don't know?"

Tian looked at her and put her hand on Ruby's shoulder.

"We are not barbarians Ruby, or above the law. As I have told you before, it is only as a last resort that I have had to kill someone, usually in self-defence or because they were causing harm to others. The likes of Feliks and the 'moles' that posed a problem in MI6 do not represent our organisation. They are gone. You can rest assured that your colleagues will look after you and provide assistance when and as needed. Without us, Great Britain and the world would be overrun with international criminals and terrorists."

Ruby thought about her father and the ex-Legionnaires who bravely backed her up when she was in trouble.

"I'm sorry Tian."

They walked further, along more corridors and down more staircases. Ruby stopped and seemed confused.

"I just have one more question to ask . . . about the fact that your father, Mister Tan is a senior figure at the Chinese embassy and the two of you seem to get help from their diplomats as part of some kind of 'second force'. And . . .

only three years ago, you were working for the Chinese Government."

"Ah yes, I was wondering when you would wake up to that one Ruby. Well, let me just say, that Britain and China once had territorial ties, especially Hong Kong, and that many Chinese diplomats from the past still associate within a 'band of brethren'. I think that is the term you use. A bit like the 'Jacko crew' who looked after you all the way from . . . well, now I'm guessing . . . but I will keep that one a secret between us."

Ruby stopped. She was stunned that Tian knew about Jacko and may have guessed where she had gone on her trip. The big surprise was that along with Mister Tan and MI6, Tian aspired to the same inter-relationship ideology as herself.

"So you were like a double-agent all along Tian. How fascinating . . . You . . . a rogue element in a rigid ideological system. Was it a difficult decision to change sides and work for the British Government?"

"Well, I didn't come here to start up a Chinese Takeaway. Anyway, enough said Ruby. We all have secrets to protect us from life's little problems. Let go of the past and move on. It is not about you . . . or me, or 'C' who decides whether you feel comfortable staying in this organisation. It is about stopping the next terrorist attack and countering the festering of hate within our own borders. It is about protecting families . . . including yours."

Tian pointed to Ruby's photo security-tag and the coat of arms, prodding her lightly.

"This is you Ruby Peters and this is what you stand for. Now get over the emotion, the worry, the fear . . . and start making a difference with everything you have. We need you girl. From today, you have a chance to make a difference. Give us one hundred per cent and your trust . . . or go home."

Ruby felt empowered with a sense of belonging - albeit to multiple factions. It was later that day when thinking about the trip to Blackpool that she realised that Jacko could not have looked at

Davis's papers and so had obviously not told MI6 about their existence. She also presumed that Tian would have known about Jacko anyway, as he had helped Davis in the past and so most certainly would have worked out where she had gone.

Davis did mention in his letter that he had left nothing for Tian "because she can look after herself." That left Ruby to consider that she was in a unique position.

She had the backing of them all if needed.

New Start

During the first few days of her new job, Ruby was involved with no less than five lengthy induction meetings. Each one covered a unique part of her workplace, authorising her to move around various classified areas at Vauxhall Cross.

As a Grade Three FIO, she had access to the standard munitions allocation area and some operations control rooms, as well as the general meeting rooms and administrative staff areas.

She managed to catch the curious gaze of 'C' once on his travels. He had looked a bit miffed at first, angry about her refusal to come clean on any news of Davis's papers, but he did seem to have other, more pressing issues on his mind. At their two-minute meeting, she sensed that at least he was getting used to her ways.

> "Welcome aboard Ruby. I will arrange to give you your first real assignment, later in the week. So until then, please make sure to restrain yourself from kicking or annoying anybody. Oh . . . and the next time you see that white poodle at your apartment, please recover our 'series 3' listening device. We're not made of money you know."

They both stared at each other briefly before 'C' was spirited away by a senior military officer and the defence minister. They looked quite edgy. Other military uniforms were busily scurrying around operations room '2 Delta K'. The door slammed closed with two keenly alert agents standing guard. Nothing was left to chance.

On the Friday morning, Ruby was summoned to her first training session since graduation, followed by a meeting with John Coltridge and his team of FIOs. She was issued with a gaudy travel bag during her munitions induction, with instructions to 'always keep it close-by' when they travelled on fieldwork. As an initial training exercise, they had to tote it around twenty-four hours a day for two days, as they went about their normal business.

Ruby did not like the bag at all. Wrong colour, funny shape and too plain, for how she would normally outfit herself. The men had a plain brown man-bag, which also clipped to their belts. They did not care what it looked like – they looked awful . . . and the bags.

It did not take long for Ruby to start up her usual cheery conversation with the somewhat 'hyperactive' trainer, Jack Carlton.

"Can we move the contents from this old bag into one of our own? It stands out too much and is too heavy."

The other two women at the session agreed with Ruby and soon started a lively debate of the issue, which really annoyed the trainer.

"Yes, you can. Of course you can move the contents into one of your own bags . . . but then the bloody fancy gadgets that you have in there will not get charged up by the bloody charging device, that is built into that particular bloody bag," he shouted back angrily.

Ruby looked surprised at his sudden rise to full-on rage.

"Well I only thought that for surveillance work, the aim is to look normal and blend in with what people expect us to be wearing. This bag is hideous. No woman would be seen dead with a bag like that."

Carlton thought for a moment, rubbing his chin.

"I agree with you there . . . that's because a women with a bag like that would be alive, thanks to its contents. You will learn all about that forthwith. OK? Anyone else not satisfied with their clothes, hair . . . shoes?"

Ruby decided to keep quiet for the rest of the session as everyone was staring at her. The trainer walked towards the whiteboard.

"So, without any further comment . . . take off your designer bags and place them in front of you . . . but do not play with any of the contents, until the end of this induction. I would hate to see anyone . . . anyone, have an unfortunate accident," whispered the trainer, turning to look at Ruby.

They were all hoping that Ruby would succumb to kick him in the shin, sometime during the remainder of the training. However, everything went smoothly and the training finished without further incident. In fact, everyone was impressed with their very latest 'bag of tricks' . . . and with Ruby's somewhat improved attitude.

After the session, a few people left the room, whilst four new ones joined Ruby for the FIO meeting. Ruby threw her bag into the seat near the back of the room.

Suddenly, a tall military-type man rushed into the room and immediately started to talk loudly above the idle chitchat that had developed, as if there was nobody else in the room.

> "Welcome everyone. My name is John Coltridge, head of FIO Global. Many of you know each other, but for the benefit of those who do not, please just give your name and title as we go around the room . . . starting with you . . . Bill."

> "Bill Ovens, FIO Australia."

> "Walter Plessey, FIO Indonesia."

> "Ray Appleton, FIO Singapore."

> "Reggie Baker, FIO Hong Kong."

> "Adam Sikorski, Head of FIO Australasia."

> "Stewart Thomas, FIO Australia."

> "Jenni Soames, FIO Australia."

> "Ruby Peters, FIO . . . well, just started actually."

There was a small chuckle from the group and a quick wave from Jennifer Soames, the Scottish lass who had graduated with her.

> "Ah yes, welcome to our FIO team Ruby. I am sure that the other team members can fill you in on what we do and how we travel when going overseas . . . in this case, to Australia. I am pleased to see you have been issued with your survival travel bags, full of goodies and . . ."

> "Australia? I wasn't told that I was going to Australia," interrupted Ruby, looking around the room.

> "Well then Agent Peters. You are going to Australia. How's that then?" replied Coltridge with raised eyebrows, "Now then everyone, please sit down for your briefing."

Coltridge pulled up the presentation on the video screen with the title 'Annual FIO Gathering Australasia – Brisbane, Pine Gap and Canberra'. The table of contents looked like a shopping list for totally unrelated abbreviations.

Ruby felt like walking out, only she couldn't, reasoning that it was part of the job as a Field Intelligence Operative, to actually go into the field, but she had only just started and was looking forward to sitting behind a nice desk for the first few months. She could flick through some interesting data - to get a feel for the job. She had even chosen some nice lunch places, to catch up with friends and to do some shopping too.

Suddenly a bright light popped into her thoughts.

"Brisbane . . . Australia," she murmured.

It was an excellent opportunity to check out the Davis holdings that was now hers. She imagined sneaking away during the conference week to view her property and the flash car that was waiting for her. The boat near Hobart in Tasmania would have to wait, along with the scattering of Davis's ashes from Mount Wellington, which she knew would be a bit harder to manage.

"Did you get all that Ruby?" snapped Coltridge, after seeing her smiling with her eyes closed, "You are not to comment on the people or their methods when visiting each of the venues. We are their guests. They are our partners. Thankfully those blighters do not work here with us, let me tell you."

"Oh quite . . . yes sir, I got all that . . . blighters."

Ruby got the impression that her new work colleagues were in some sort of indoctrination process, similar to joining the army. First, they strip away your identity by doing lots of training and brainwashing, and then they make you compliant to anything they want - Australia today, then the dark corners of some murderous third-world regime the next.

She looked down at her security pass – the code DH-F-18409 stared back at her. She was now just a number, with an ugly handbag and a ticket to Australia, far removed from her life in England. It was a one-way ticket too . . . hopefully an oversight.

"We can all go shopping together on the Gold Coast Ruby and head to the beach too, if it's warm enough," whispered Jenni during the break.

Ruby's thoughts returned to reality.

"Yeah, that sounds great Jenni. I also want to catch up with an old friend in Brisbane – from my school days. I hear it is always hot up there . . . and sometimes very sticky."

"That's right, usually in summer. I have been assigned to work in Canberra for a year. Now there's a basin of hot and cold extremes – not unlike Edinburgh. One of the other graduates is going to the Hobart Antarctic Conference to 'feel out' the foreign scientists who pretend to do research."

"Really? Oh my god . . . Hobart? Wow, I've got to get that gig Jenni. I just love penguins and polar bears and . . ."

"Aye yer daft cat . . . not many polar bears in Hobart, Ruby," laughed Jenni quietly.

Their smirking brought them to the attention of Coltridge, who gave them both a stern look of disapproval before continuing with his presentation. However, a message on his communicator interrupted the situation.

Things were starting to look up for Ruby. The FIO jaunt would see her able to discover her new house and car. Then, if she could extend her trip . . . well, she was in Australia after all, so there was the prospect of seeing her boat. What a great trip it would be, she thought - without any danger or undercover action. Her only duty would be to liaise with foreign counterparts and make friends with some of them. After all, they would be providing information to each other in the future. Then there was the shopping.

When the session resumed, Coltridge put up a colourful diagram with many interconnecting arrows.

"Right then, here is the inter-agency communications currently in use. You may notice that we have green, red and grey sections, representing intelligence-gathering nodes. The green is for positive reliable information coming from the CIA and ASIS agencies . . . and I say that with some sarcasm. The red areas mean that the information is doubtful, downright unreliable and possibly even fake news. Welcome to the spy industry. Anyway, that is what most information collected from that rabble entails . . . but it is all done for a purpose. We do the same of course. It's called strategic diplomacy."

He waited . . . and waited, tapping at the grey area on the diagram, until Ruby offered to complete his trifecta of whimsical data channels. She felt the need to help him out.

"What do the grey areas and lines represent sir? Are they some kind of future prospecting, or an unknown?"

"Actually, they are of sorts. Yes Ruby, nice pickup. The grey area represents information currently anticipated, but what we cannot yet obtain. We know it exists but the Yanks and the Aussies have their own strange bloody arrangement. Pine Gap handles all their communications, eavesdropping and military data for them . . . and we use it too, occasionally for what it's worth. That is why in your field bags you have a specially scrambled communicator. It uses a deciphering code only used by GCHQ. We do need to have some privacy at times . . . right Ruby?"

Ruby guessed he was hinting at her recent covert trip to Blackpool but then remembered the time GCHQ could not even decipher the simple diagram from Davis or the coded clues exposing the four 'moles', etched onto one of her diamonds.

It was only after Eric had worked it all out and told everyone, that GCHQ came out with the 'official' answer. She always wondered how he would have operated within MI6, with his free-natured, intuitive mind. She laughed to herself, knowing that Eric would have worn them out.

When the meeting was over, Coltridge asked Ruby to stay back to discuss another matter.

"Now then Ruby, there is just a small item that needs to be sorted . . . and which we will back you up . . . one hundred per cent. That bloody incident with the infamous diamonds and those two CIA agents who were trying to steal them has raised its head yet again," he muttered quickly.

"I thought that was all sorted. The Chinese got the diamonds . . . three years ago. The CIA stole them from Scarab. He was blown to bits by their own bloody drone. What more is there to tell? I mean, the two agents involved are bloody dead. I do not have to tell you that. They died the same day as Davis and I have tried to forget about all that. Why is that an issue now? What the hell is wrong with those bloody clowns? What else do they want from me? Will I be armed when I see them? I could throw my stupid bloody bag at them."

Coltridge looked at her tensing up. Even he felt uncomfortable at raising the issue and pursuing it further.

"Look, the CIA only want you to formally identify the two agents that were on that boat from their files, so that the case can be closed. That is all. Yes, true, they stole the diamonds from Scarab but the CIA say that through your actions, the diamonds were taken from their operatives, albeit rogue agents . . . and ended up . . . well, I think we confiscated them in the end as treasure . . . if I remember the Navy report correctly."

"Yes, then they were given to the Chinese government in exchange for preventing another bloody international incident . . . a certain matter of entrapment comes to mind. We should have given the diamonds back to the CIA. I have a good mind to tell them a few home truths and kick them where it hurts . . . stupid bastards. They are only mad because the diamonds were to be used to pay someone else. Bloody money laundering bastards that's all they are . . . operating outside of their guidelines again no doubt, to finance more mayhem around the world."

"Yes, quite, calm down there Ruby and mind your swearing. That is not our concern anyway. All we want is for you to identify the agents involved and then Adam Sikorski will sign you out of the dispute for all time. We are not blaming you at all Ruby, but we need your assurance that you will identify the agents and sign the papers. Then we can all move on. That lot do deals and operations completely without authority I know, but it is in our interest to keep them on-side. That comes from the very top by the way. "C" has been briefed by the PM himself and the matter mustl be finalised without any repercussions from either side. Unfortunately, we still need their help at times."

Ruby was in no position to argue. She was seething inside after taking all the risk for the government's incompetence. At least, the proposed meeting with the CIA would put another loose end to bed.

"I want to be protected when I do this just in case there are any further complications. I do not trust the Americans after what I have seen and heard. Surely, you could have handled it from our offices here in England?"

"No Ruby, they wanted a neutral country."

"Like Australia is bloody neutral right? They depend on America for all their security and have a Teflon foreign policy. We now seem to be doing much the same too, by the way. Talking about bloody weapons of mass destruction . . . stirring up trouble around the bloody world."

"Now look here Ruby. We steer well clear of politics here. It is not 'speaker's corner'. When you get there, keep your thoughts to yourself and just do what they have asked. Simply view, recognise, sign and leave. OK? You are representing the United Kingdom . . . not Ruby Enterprises Unlimited . . . OK?"

Ruby mumbled something inaudible ending in 'sir' as she headed towards the door. The other FIOs had gathered outside to hear her fiery words, catching a glimpse of 'C' disappearing down the corridor with a wry smile on his face. She presumed he must have been listening at the door to her foreign policy.

"You'll not transform me into your 'maid-servant'," whispered Ruby, screwing up her nose.

Airport Security

Ruby packed her shiny red suitcase during the afternoon before the midnight flight from Heathrow to Western Australia. As she was selecting her clothes, most of which resided all over the bedroom and lounge floors, it suddenly dawned on her that she still had to carry that hideous handbag around at all times. It was most certainly a tracking device and it would be 'grounded' the moment her 'working day' finished, leaving them to think that she was in her hotel room. She threw it into the suitcase and stared at it for a while.

She was dreading the long-haul flight of seventeen hours with no stopovers and already felt tired and irritable, which made her think about the blueberry muffin sitting all alone in the fridge. Then a call came through.

"Hello, who's calling?"

"It's me, Tian. Just wanting to know that you are 'ready to go' for your trip down under. Just remember to get some sleep on the plane. You will have to go all day at the other end you know. All a planned part of the course, made to test all new graduates into keeping alert and focussed."

"What . . . while we are sleeping? Really Tian, who thought up that little gem? Anyway, sleeping in economy class is like being sent to the bloody knacker's yard on an old rag-and-bone truck . . . and you know how that always turns out."

"Anyway, just thought I'd call to see how you are."

"Grumpy! Put that in your report . . . and tell 'C' that I am in a most disagreeable mood . . . you know . . . the kind that may lead to an altercation of some sort."

"Come on Ruby. I really think you need to take up some active competitive sport instead of that lazy gym workout you do. Such as . . . Rugby, Kickboxing . . . something aggressive, that gets all that pent-up energy out of you."

"Ha! I saw you spying on me the other day at my gym, sneaking around the foyer in your leggings. Well I may actually get back to doing my karate again. It's always great wiping the floor with someone much bigger than me."

"Unless they also know karate, then that would be rather foolish and pointless. Oh, I can see the old Ruby coming to the fore. Anyway, I have to go . . . got a lunch across the river."

"You wait until you see my expenses. Ha! Goodbye Tian, enjoy your lettuce leaf and wafer biscuit."

Ruby remembered the sumptuous spread for lunch served at the Morpeth Arms across the bridge from MI6, washed down with Cab Sav and maybe a strong black coffee to keep the eyes open for the remainder of the lazy afternoon.

She checked her itinerary, calculating her arrival at midday in Perth the next day for a one-night rest at the Rendezvous Hotel on the surf coast. On closer inspection, with correction to the Perth time zone, it was now painfully obvious that it would be after midnight when she arrived. That left a window of six hours before she had to meet with some local agent in the foyer before returning to the airport, for a flight to Darwin. She would have to endure a further four hours of more in cattle-class travel.

Although travelling under her real name to a 'friendly' country, she was well aware that the Australians would be conducting baggage inspections and identity checks at every opportunity, to see what 'interesting' items she was carrying. Every Australian agency would be on training and surveillance duties looking for those irritating 'pommy agents', in order to avoid any embarrassing incidents. The Americans would be paranoid about having nine FIOs visit their bases, at the same time. They apparently run their bases as if they are on American soil – a sure sign of authority.

Because Ruby was working for MI6, visiting highly sensitive areas of national security and meeting with their security personnel, everyone expected her to be hustling for information and contacts. It was time to hide any 'things' that could be filmed or 'lifted' and they wanted to know where Ruby went, who she met and why - at all times. They had a dossier two feet thick on her meddling into things that did not concern her.

As nine FIOs were going in pairs on different flights to Perth, Ruby wondered who would be sharing her flight. She imagined that John Coltridge would prefer to travel on his own and probably always flew first class anyway.

Arriving at the busy Heathrow terminal by taxi, Ruby made her way to the Qantas security check-in. It was a cold, rainy night and she would have preferred to be tucked-up in her warm bed.

"Good evening. Ruby Peters . . . I am travelling to Perth on your flight QF9."

"Good evening Ruby. Welcome aboard your Qantas experience. Just the one case today?"

"That's right . . . and my hand luggage too. I like your accent by the way. Where are you from in Australia?"

"I am from Adelaide originally and then worked in Melbourne and Sydney for a while. I've taken on this London location for a change, so I can see Europe."

"That's great. Plenty to see in the UK too, you know. I'm going to Brisbane, Darwin and Pine . . . and Perth of course."

"Well you're on the right flight then. Have a nice trip to Australia Ruby. Make your way to boarding gate 3 through security over there."

Ruby smiled and checked out her surroundings. She was used to being in constant surveillance mode at all times, looking for cameras, security personnel, suspicious people and baggage and . . . she felt that inner sense of being followed again. She put on her glasses to examine the boarding pass, checking the reflection behind her and to each side . . . nothing obvious.

It was too busy to recognise anyone out of place, so she made her way to the security scanners. Some of the airport staff looked at her more closely than at any other passenger. Some were in plain clothes giving fleeting glances, secretive nods to their mates, or lingering last looks at her clothes, hand luggage and facial expression.

"Excuse me, but would you mind stepping to one side please."

The young security officer gingerly touched her shoulder and proceeded to move the 'wand' over her arms, front and shoes, whilst he nervously explained the purpose of the act.

"This scanner is testing for traces of explosives, chemicals and any illicit drugs . . . quite normal for a random check."

"That's fine if you are not a junkie or terrorist. Have you been doing this long?"

The officer did not answer and was immune to her smile as he inserted the wand into the analyser. Ruby was annoyed as the officer stared at the screen for quite a while, almost as though he was 'willing it' to produce some devastating information.

"Won't be long now. It takes a few seconds to . . . there, that's fine, thank you," he said on turning his back on her.

"Well done. That wasn't so hard Einstein," she murmured, but he was already walking away.

The baggage x-ray staff at least showed more interest in her, although some appeared a little too alert.

"Put your keys, belt buckle, coins and mobile phone on this tray, separate to your bag," barked a sharp young woman with a voice like a snappy Chihuahua.

Ruby threw her goods into the tray and slid it along the conveyor with some force so that it hit the curtain at an angle. Entering the personal detector gate, she walked through fast and furious.

"You win. Now can you please go back and try that again," smiled the man with a casual attitude, at the other end.

"Sure . . . same speed or what? Should I take off my metal leg?"

The young man walked through the detector slowly, with a bit of a wiggle, to show her how it was done. He waited, watching her mumbling something, and shook his head.

"See. Even a fellow colleague can do it . . . Ruby Peters. You don't remember me do you? I still have a bruise where you kicked me during training. Jack Parton. Yes, I did actually graduate too by the way," he beamed.

Ruby looked at him closely as the other staff just frowned and raised their eyebrows. He looked different, smarter and efficient with his shorter hair and a uniform.

"Jack! Well, well, well. The ambitiously amorous training partner who met his match. I kicked you twice actually."

"Yes, well it was all playtime back then and now like you I'm just so enthralled by these unfamiliar surroundings. They do hate us you know – bloody customs bogies. At least you are travelling . . . and I am stuck here. The perks of being a Grade 3, I suppose. Do I salute or what?"

The security area was now quite busy, held up by Jack and his memories, and Ruby's obstreperous attitude. The detector and x-ray carousel were at a standstill. A burly security officer arrived like an armoured tank, to see who or what was holding up his 'pax processing' area.

"Jack. Get your bloody arse back on the job and stop irritating the passengers with your unprofessional behaviour."

Ruby was walking away as Jack stared at her, unconcerned and with a wide grin remembering how he had tackled her in training, restraining her, with his face pressed up against hers. He was now on official MI6 duties and not part of that lower echelon airport and customs fraternity.

Walking into the boarding area, Ruby had worked out her 'tail' after seeing a young woman loitering nervously around the check-in, now held up by the queue. Ruby's ploy for creating a disturbance at security had flushed her out. She smiled and screwed up her nose.

Ruby continued to mingle in with the crowd, evading the woman as she walked towards the newsagents. Her distinctive American accent and that intermittent alert look about her, gave her away as being most definitely CIA. The standard procedure to 'ignore the tail' and either 'lose it or keep it at a distance', did not sit well with Ruby.

"Hey there! Don't I know you from somewhere?"

The young woman looked flustered and dropped her credit card. They both reached down to retrieve it, eyeing each other up.

"I noticed you all the way through the airport and thought that maybe we had met before . . . possibly in the same industry. You know – Intel Corporation," whispered Ruby.

"Well, really I don't think so. I . . . I'm an art teacher – in a school."

"Really . . . and that familiar earpiece . . . is that a work of art? I have exactly the same model. See, Motorola knows no bounds in marketing their spyware it seems."

The woman reminded Ruby of her naïve self, three years ago on her first assignment for Davis. They both looked at each other as they stood up, realising that they looked uncannily similar, with the same colour coat, hair colour, height.

"Matching twins. You know I can't say anything, but it is common practice to follow other agents around before meeting with them in a foreign country. Nice coat by the way," whispered the woman without moving her lips.

"And how do you find the work . . . Cathy?"

"But how . . . how the hell do you know my name? I have only just started. Are you part of my damn training?"

"Nope. I would never work for your lot in a million years. No, I just pointed my trusty lapel camera and used my said earpiece . . . and a whacking big database at GCHQ sprang into life. You lady . . . are on our books."

They both relaxed, as Ruby patted her shoulder, pretending to offer friendship, placing a 'device' on her coat.

"Hi, I'm Ruby."

"Yes I know!"

"Oh, right of course you do. So now, I think we should just merge back into the background Cathy. Maybe see you in Perth?"

"How did you know that?"

"Your boarding pass is showing Cathy. Here . . . take this magazine to read on the plane."

Ruby smiled as she walked away to get a coffee, feeling very calm and proud of her honed skills. She had not noticed the middle-aged person in plain casual clothes, wearing a neat jacket, standing near the bookshop wall. This person was not smiling . . . or doing anything to attract attention.

> "This is a Qantas announcement. Flight QF9 leaving for Perth, Western Australia is now ready for boarding from gate three. Please make your way to the boarding gate now."

Ruby watched the people milling towards the exit gate and reached for her boarding pass. Suddenly, there was a loud scream and a crowd started gathering around the Newsagents. There was an immediate rush of armed security personnel running to the area. Ruby could see some of the crowd turning away, looking shocked and upset.

> "This is a Qantas announcement. Flight QF9 leaving for Perth, Western Australia is now ready for boarding from gate three. Please make your way to the boarding gate now."

Ruby hesitated, and then went over to have a look at what was going on. Jack Parton was there too, rising up from the floor. He caught a glimpse of Ruby and his face looked ashen. She had seen such a foreboding look many times before. It was not a good sign.

> "Ruby, get on your plane right now and don't ask any questions or look at the body."

> "Body, but what has happened Jack? I want to have a look. Does it concern me at all? I mean I'm just a tourist catching a plane, right?"

> "Stay away and catch your flight. I'll handle this . . . it's going to be a major incident, being in a public place. Go, now."

Ruby caught a glimpse of a young woman, completely still, lying there, with someone who was possibly a doctor checking her eyes . . . a familiar magazine was clutched in her hand. Ruby was stunned and she was also in the way of paramedics who pushed her roughly to one side without a word. Within a few seconds, the looks on the faces of the paramedics confirmed Ruby's darkest thoughts.

> "Let's get her to the holding area mate . . . an ambulance is on the way."

Jack flashed his ID and waited for a response from Mike, the senior paramedic.

"Sorry, but there's nothing more we can do this time."

"Right, ok then Mike. Thanks for your help. I'll follow you down and we'll speak some more about the 'process'."

Jack could see Ruby staring at the lifeless Cathy as she bent down to secretly retrieve her 'device'. Jack put a hand on her shoulder, slowly but forcibly moving her away, steering her towards the near empty line of boarding passengers.

"Nothing to do with you at all Ruby It's just a medical emergency with an unfortunate outcome."

"And the knife wound Jack?"

He did not answer. He was busy scouring the area for clues and checking the camera angles for possible visuals. Ruby joined the trail end of the queue for boarding.

"Welcome aboard . . . Ruby. Thank you for flying with us today. We hope you enjoy your flying experience."

The flight attendant was blissfully unaware of what had just happened or why Ruby was wiping away a forming tear.

As Ruby walked through the departure gate, the middle-aged person moved quickly towards the toilet area, talking on an encrypted phone to inform the boss that they had killed the wrong person. There was a brief reply before being cut-off.

"You failed me with your incompetence. Get on that plane and finish the job. Your ticket is valid only for this flight. We will make further arrangements. Don't fail me again."

The person quickly ripped off the facial build-up and wig applied earlier, adding some glasses then turning the well-cut, mid-length, dark grey jacket inside out, before running to the boarding gate.

"Welcome aboard. You have only just made it in time. I hope you have a pleasant trip and don't get bothered too much. I've put you in seat number 17F to stretch your legs."

The security team had already analysed the visual data from the cameras as the plane waited in the holding bay on orders directly from MI6. There was a person of interest who did not appear on any entry cameras to the airport. They were still looking. They did not catch flight QF9 either . . . or apparently any other flight.

Jack was worried about Ruby's safety, frantically checking all the toilet cubicles for the assailant and for any other clues hidden in the waste bins. He found nothing of interest.

"The murderer is either still in the airport or is on one of six flights that have just taken off. I think it was mistaken identity Dave. They did wear very similar outfits . . . our Ruby and Cathy. It was Ruby they wanted. The murderer must have had a good disguise."

"Thanks Jack. We will watch out for Ruby. In fact, get on that plane now. We will hold it for you. You will be her shadow. Ruby will trust you if you both get exposed to any further danger . . . and then while you're at it, maybe you can charm her into finding out if she is hiding anything about one of our agents . . . killed in action."

"What agent . . . when?"

"Roger Davis, about three years ago. He was one of the best agents we ever had."

"Davis . . . yes I know quite a bit about his life and his missions. It is not very comforting to realise that a new graduate like me with no experience, has to be very sceptical about living a long life," replied Jack.

"Forever young Jack . . . remember that song? It was written for us mate. Do you really want to live forever Jack?"

Close Quarters

Ruby sat in the window seat next to the emergency door, overlooking the wing. She was relieved that nobody had taken up the middle seat that was next to her. The aisle seat remained empty too, as the main cabin door closed . . . and then opened again. The other passengers had not noticed or had picked up that the flight attendants seemed edgy. The crew had necessarily been told of the murder and that their plane was still on-hold, until an 'official' could travel with them.

Suddenly, a young man raced into the doorway, scaring the attendant, flashing his security pass and a wide smile before pulling up and then calmly walking down the aisle. He sat down and turned towards Ruby.

"Hi there, Jack's the name. I am the reserve pilot, just taking some time out to read the dinner menu and it seems that we are short on wings but there are plenty of breasts."

"Jack! What are you doing here? Have you not got more important things to do?"

"Well, that's a start. Yes, I'm very well, thank you."

"Look, I don't need a bloody nurse maid on my first overseas assignment."

"No, no, of course not. I am on a separate assignment Ruby. I have been told to track down the person who got to Cathy. There is a remote possibility that he could be on this flight, but I doubt that."

"Or her Jack. You really didn't learn much."

Jack had not considered that at all but he did not let on.

"Well that makes you a suspect too then, doesn't it smarty pants. There were no kick marks on her though. Anyway, I was ordered to get on this plane and to keep my eyes open. There was no time to rally the troops, and six of us had to catch different flights. I will probably have to fly straight back on the next plane after a day off of course . . . unless something exciting happens. Mind you, I have no luggage or change of clothes."

Ruby was now kind of half-listening to his rambling. She scoured the passengers around her – covertly of course, but they all looked the same . . . tired and overwhelmed at the thought of spending seventeen hours in a cigar tube.

"The Americans aren't going to like this outcome one bit. You know that she was following me, don't you Jack? I spoke to her briefly . . . so naïve and poorly trained. The other thing is Jack, she looked a hell of a lot like me - similar coat, hair. That was supposed to be me back there Jack. Someone wants to kill me . . . and I have no idea why."

Jack stared at Ruby with her incredibly simple explanation. He wondered if this was his opportunity to find out if she was hiding anything. He moved to the middle seat and sat back with his eyes closed and then looked at her sideways.

"It's like this Ruby. You have been involved with some pretty nasty customers since joining the 'company' and there are many reasons why some of them would want to see you out of the way . . . but you and I both know, that Davis is the key to all of this. You keep getting yourself targeted only because of your association with him and his previous missions."

"What do you mean? Roger is dead. All that business is over and done with. It has been three years . . . three long years, so don't start telling me that he is to blame. I won't have it Jack."

"And the loose ends Ruby? There is no evidence of his will or financial papers or family connections . . . nothing. There are people on all sides wanting to know what information he left behind . . . you know . . . in case of his sudden departure . . . and there you are, playing your own silly game yet again."

Ruby sighed and looked away before snapping back.

"Well, it's obvious that 'C' has found himself yet another stooge to follow me around, just like Tian - only in it for the information and the notoriety of getting the better of me when I'm in trouble. Not actually giving me any help."

"You're wrong Ruby . . . about me anyway. Personally, I think 'trouble' is your middle name. Sure, I was told to follow you on this flight. Yes, and even to find out what you know, but like you, I am my own person. You have to keep something of yourself in reserve in this job just to stay sane. I like to see what the real reasons are for what I am ordered to do. I do have a conscience you know . . . and a strong willingness to survive. Unlike bloody Roger Davis . . . the best operative they ever had . . . until he proved them wrong."

"What are you saying Jack?"

"Look, someone of Davis's standing rarely slip-up or get duped into relaxing their guard. It is usually someone close, very close, someone beyond reproach that you would never expect, who does them in. There are many examples of such folly amongst international agents . . . and then there is internal resentment . . . and the curse of the double agent."

Ruby was stunned but it did get her thinking along the same lines, if only for a moment.

"What would you know about him anyway and who do you think would betray him at close quarters?" she asked, watching for any further clues as to his allegiance.

"I actually studied him as part of my training. I mean he was the best of the best Ruby . . . I even wanted to be like him. I am a lot like him, wanting a chance to make things right in the world. You cannot have close friends or relationships in a job like ours, or drag other people into our world . . . a world of such violence. It is not a life for someone with a family. Anyway, I studied him in detail . . . and you were a part of that too. You can't keep courting trouble for yourself . . . and others."

It was hard for Ruby to respond to his thoughts.

"If you studied me, then you would know that I was recruited prematurely, just a vulnerable schoolgirl trying to find my way . . . and I've never experienced a quiet moment since. Really Jack, you are just a persistent stalker."

"Oh, I studied the situations that you were in and somehow managed to survive . . . most of them by shear good fortune and not skill, as far as I can see. I believe Tian saved your skin on at least three occasions. I also know about the foreign legion connection that your dad and Eric's dad shared too but I can only guess what must go on in your head . . . especially after all that personal tragedy and betrayal of trust. So now, you know about my situation and what I know about you. I will take what I deem to be of importance and act on it, but only when necessary. So do not tell me anything that you may regret, because I will use it as I see fit. Fair warning and all that."

"Ha, nice try Jack. I can see that you are more suited to an auction house. I will give you fair warning too Jack, about our disreputable industry and the likes of Roger Davis, which you are not by the way. Never trust anyone, anything or even the illusions of a reality that you may even think exists. You can only live for the moment, and if you think that is not possible . . . then be wary of your enemies throughout the remainder of time and space. Good always triumphs over evil if you choose the right people. Goodnight and pleasant dreams Jack. Now get back to your own seat if you know what is good for you. Fair warning indeed."

Jack moved back to the aisle seat as Ruby settled in for a long sleep, still thinking about what Jack had said about betrayal by a close friend. She wondered if Tian had played any part in informing Jack about her probable 'day trip' to Blackpool.

Jack looked sideways at her and smiled to himself. She looked so beautiful, warm and vulnerable . . . on the outside at least. He now had a strong feeling that she had Davis's personal papers. He grinned at the thought of being with Ruby for the next seventeen hours, thinking back to when she had taken his breath away, lying side by side during training. He wanted to stroke her hair and . . .

Ruby quickly turned towards Jack. He was still staring at her.

"Owwww, what was that for?"

"That's three times now, pervert," replied Ruby, before returning to her sleeping position.

Jack decided it was time to get some sleep too. With the low frequency hum of the engines and minimal lighting, it was quite easy to doze off, which put paid to the myth that an agent is supposedly alert for any emergency or a sudden change in their surroundings.

Most agents would reluctantly agree that their work was little more than that of a journalist – collecting information, looking for leads and anomalies, and following up information and people to see what fits in with other known facts.

Ruby had a different slant on that – she had been through such intense action that most agents would never likely experience in a lifetime, making her always half-awake. It only extended the waking time available to dwell on her fear of never finding inner peace.

The crew prepared to serve the main meal. The aroma of cooked food and fresh coffee brought Ruby and Jack to their sitting positions. They eyed each other off, while fidgeting with their tables, magazines and clothing.

"So, it looks like dinner is on its way. I'm starved and I didn't pick up anything before I left," said Jack briskly.

"I had a burger and thick shake at 10 o'clock but I'm still hungry. It's the cold night air and being out of the normal daily cycle that does it. Anyway did you have a good nap?" replied Ruby trying to be cheery.

"Oh, off and on, what with the sore leg. What about you? I hope you managed to put that encounter with Cathy out of your mind . . . and my comments about . . . you know, studying you and all that. Anyway, I will be gone after this flight Ruby . . . so we may as well keep on good terms. I mean, we are 'company', and on a free flight."

Ruby nodded and screwed her nose up.

"Yep, that's true and we graduated together at the same time and are both now facing the reality of travelling alone as FIOs. Sorry about the leg and everything."

Jack suspected Ruby was refocussing on her mission.

"Cathy Summers," announced Jack, watching her reaction.

"What?"

"Cathy Summers, aged twenty three . . . used to be an art teacher at a primary school before apparently signing up with the CIA graduate intake. She did some bit part acting too."

"So she was an art teacher after all. What a terrible outcome from working in a safe primary school with little children. Such a different world apart from this," replied Ruby.

"Well . . . unless the primary school is in America . . . bloody gun-mad people. Anyway, she was assigned to follow you around as part of this conference business you are going to. Just playing out the part, so I am told. The Americans like to keep their new agents on their toes and send them to other countries as soon as possible, to monitor how they handle themselves in different surroundings, different cultures . . . and without backup," continued Jack briskly.

"What else do you know Jack, and why wasn't I briefed after Cathy's death? . . . So, was she the target . . . or me, Jack?"

Jack looked at her carefully. He leaned across to her and whispered.

"You have something that many people would die for . . . will die for . . . having secreted the private papers and financial portfolio of Roger Davis into your apparently precious life."

"And why would you think that Jack?"

"I don't think that at all Ruby. I know you have them . . . as does 'C' . . . as does the CIA and all those nasty little terrorist grubs now surfacing from wars long gone. You, Ruby Peters are hot property . . . and many people want to put you out, permanently."

Ruby looked away, thinking quickly about her situation and the toll it had taken on her family. She reached over to him and pulled his tie tight.

"Anything else you want to run by me Jack? Do you want to know what I think? I think you are all bluffing and with good reason. I don't have anything. Nothing . . . except a sad private letter written by Roger, to apologise for recruiting me and Eric . . . and also to tell me, not to trust anyone . . . anyone, especially nosey bloody colleagues."

Jack sighed and sank into his seat as Ruby let go.

"Are you having dinner today," asked the flight attendant reaching over to Ruby.

"Yes please. I'll have the roast beef and Yorkshire pudding and a strong drink," replied Ruby, now annoyed that Jack was smiling again, having transferred his short attention span to the over-extended flight attendant.

"And who are you having for dinner Jack!" she snapped.

"What?"

Touch Down

QF9 made a perfect touchdown at Perth International Airport. Most people were still too tired to know whether to feel excited or just plain relieved. Some had interconnecting flights to Melbourne and Sydney. They were the ones who looked most annoyed.

> "Welcome to Perth and thank you for flying Qantas. The time is now 1 am local time – a little later than normal due to the headwind. We were also waiting for clearance to taxi back to the terminal. I hope your flight . . ."

Ruby flopped back in her seat. Out of the corner of her eye she saw Jack staring at the same flight attendant who was obviously flattered enough to keep his attention.

> "Give it a rest Jack . . . remember what you said about close friends getting in the way of your precious work . . . you know . . . to save the world?"

Jack sat back in his chair with his eyes closed and a grin.

> "I was just thinking about how that poor flight attendant just smiles at everybody . . . on every flight. While I have been sleeping here with you for seventeen hours . . ."

> "In your dreams Jack. I bet you flirt with anybody, on every flight too and . . . if you were asleep for seventeen hours as you say, then I wouldn't be bragging about it."

As the passengers stood up, rummaging around the overhead lockers, Ruby stayed seated as Jack checked everyone he could see, watching their faces, hands and hand luggage.

Finally, there was a sufficient break for Ruby and Jack to join the queue to the exit door. Jack moved into the aisle to let Ruby out.

> "See you much later Jack," said Ruby with a little wave, as she marched forward, looking over her shoulder.

> "Or in heaven Ruby . . . or in heaven, my scarlet angel," he shouted back with a laugh.

As Jack reached up to retrieve his bag, the person behind him eased into his body, pushing him into the empty seat. The remaining ten passengers walked past in a hurry to leave the plane, not noticing that the man in row 17 was holding his throat, gasping for air, unable to make a sound.

The last passenger left through the front exit door just as flight attendants noticed Jack's feet sticking out into the aisle. They rushed down to see what was wrong and on seeing Jack unconscious, raised the alarm. Another attendant joined them and with a lot of effort, dragged him into the aisle to begin resuscitation.

Security was already racing to the plane as Ruby walked towards the baggage collection area. She reactivated her earpiece and walked up to the baggage carousel, noticing that there was a flurry of activity heading for the gate from where she had just come. She imagined that Jack would not be a part of it at all, as they were now in a foreign country – albeit Australia . . . and Jack's attention would not be welcome and was probably following another flight attendant.

Suddenly, a tall burly man came from behind and stood beside her, very close . . . and then another. They were both armed and she identified their mannerisms as being airport security. They seemed to be on high alert for an incident or were trying to intimidate her.

"Get away from me or I'll scream!" shouted Ruby for all to hear.

"Ruby Peters? My name is Arthur and this is Josh . . . we are here to protect you. We are from ASIS and believe that you have been the target of two incidents. We also think that your life is in danger."

Arthur showed his security pass, followed by Josh.

"You must come with us immediately where you will be safe. We need to know who this person is. Two deaths hints at a professional hit man," continued Arthur.

"What are you talking about? What two deaths? What's going on? I want to speak to someone from my embassy. Look, I have my ID here. Look closely. I'm on my way to a bloody conference in Brisbane with your lot."

"Yes we know who you are Ruby. We have been expecting you . . . but certainly not with an entrance like this."

"I'm here with Jack . . . we caught the same flight. I have to tell him of this development. He is also in great danger," flustered Ruby, looking at the solemn ASIS officers.

Ruby saw their composure change to anguish as Arthur received a message through his earpiece. His manner became firmer as if in interrogation mode.

"That would be Jack Parton I presume, Miss Peters?"

"Yes . . . why?"

"I'd like you to come with us right now. You need to answer some questions about Jack. You were the last person to see him according to the flight attendant. You have the right to remain silent but whatever you do say, may be used in evidence against you. Do you understand?"

Ruby nodded. She was feeling gutted. The situation was all too familiar. She hesitated to ask the obvious.

"He's dead isn't he? Jack is dead. How did he die? What happened to him? He was right behind me. I cannot believe it. Jack was . . . Jack was my friend."

The two officers just stared at her, emotionless, weighing up her response. They escorted her to the security area where more officers were waiting. She felt alone and abandoned by everyone. Then her earpiece came to life.

"This is K439, Ruby. Stay put and do not answer any of their questions before I arrive to sort things out. I am sorry but Jack has been killed. Looks like the same person who killed Cathy. We are working on it. Stay calm and positive. I will be there within the hour. Do not say anything. Nothing."

Ruby managed to remove her earpiece and turn it off to prevent detection. She pushed it deep into her hair with a time delay for it to activate as a homing beacon after one hour.

The two guards steered Ruby into a small office where she they eventually gave her a coffee and some plain biscuits. One of the guards stood next to her at all times and the familiar large mirror, which was obviously a 'two-way' looked at odds with the size of the room. A man in a dark suit approached her, avoiding her eyes as he sat on the table edge. He did not introduce himself. It looked like an interrogation was starting and she still had no legal representation. The man finally looked at her, after weighing up her state of mind.

"Some things have already been cleared up Miss Peters and we are just waiting for one of your people to arrive. In the meantime, I am sorry, but we want you to identify the body as being that of Jack Parton. I know it will be difficult but our protocol demands that we clear up that matter first."

Ruby nodded and closed her eyes, wondering how she would cope seeing Jack laid out for inspection. She would also have to break the news to her family that she was involved in yet more trouble. The man in the suit walked all around her, suddenly appearing next to her right cheek.

"You . . . were the last person seen speaking with Cathy Summers and you were sitting next to Jack. She was a nice girl, Cathy . . . only a few weeks after her graduation within the CIA too. They are not at all happy with this situation, given that you are already a person of interest on their wanted list. Did you know that Miss Peters?"

"Jack told me about it on the plane. He said that he was following a suspect on my flight."

"Indeed Miss Peters . . . and may I ask you if that suspect was actually . . . yourself? It makes a lot of sense to some people, however, it would be hard for anyone to prove that now, wouldn't it . . . with both agents now deceased and yet both closely linked to you? I wonder what your MI6 will be thinking about your cursed approach to defending their values. You have quite a history Miss Peters and a trail of destruction and bodies," he replied quietly.

Ruby grabbed hold of his tie and forced his head down towards the table, making him lose his balance. The burly guard was quick to intervene, but the suited man was winded and was surprised at her quick reaction. Yet, he brushed her away quickly before regaining composure.

"You will get nothing from me until I see my embassy official. I was here on a friendly visit to meet my counterparts from ASIS and the CIA in Brisbane. Why the hell do you think that I would want to kill two innocent people, including one of our own agents . . . a friend. Bloody morons. I will report back that you have treated me badly and are acting on behalf of your American counterparts."

"Well we do not want your kind of friendship here Miss Peters and I am going to insist that you be charged immediately. You are not in bloody Pommy Land now you know. You'll get life in prison for what you've done."

"And I'll sue you for wrongful arrest and bloody harassment. What is your name anyway 'suit-man', and who or what do you represent? You could be the bloody toilet cleaner with schizophrenia with your attitude and . . ."

Just then, David Pomphrey arrived, announcing himself at the door as the British Consulate representative and demanding immediate full access to Ruby. He sounded rather posh, like a Whitehall lawyer for the establishment, which annoyed the tough-looking Australians.

"Well, I see things are off to a flying start then . . . hands across the sea and all that."

"Too right mate. Your amateur sleuth over here seems to think that killing two innocent people on our national airline is a joke. We are only conducting enquiries at present and she is being difficult, abusive . . . and violent. If she is innocent, you can have her back on the very next flight . . . but not on Qantas. She can go on a pommy plane and kill as many poms as she wants. But . . . if she's involved with these two deaths, then we will get first crack at her, through the Australian legal system and put her away for a long time."

Pomphrey had a bit of quiet sigh and made light of the situation, before turning to his duties.

"Yes, I have heard about your 'kangaroo courts', guilty until proven innocent. Anyway . . . I have here, written authority to vouch for Miss Peters, as I am authorised to take her with me . . . now. I doubt that she will be looked after too well if she stays with you and your intelligence network. So, Ruby, I am afraid that your 'friendly' trip is now cancelled. We will make other arrangements for your short stay in Australia. I believe you were here to liaise with your counterparts in ASIS and the CIA? I doubt that anyone will have anything good to say about your reception . . . or your absence from their conferences. Maybe the Americans will push for your extradition. But I will make sure this international incident is plastered all over the British tabloids if that ever happens. Is that clear?"

The Australians were a bit apprehensive about his threat.

"She's going nowhere mate until I get the proper authority from my senior colleagues. I have to follow strict procedure. Two murdered agents do not get your client a trip home on Virgin bloody airlines. Not without first being dealt with by our judicial system. You're not in 'Pommy Land' now, you pompous prick," said the suited man with a snarl.

Pomphrey calmly reached into his inner pocket to produce a document, watched on by the nervous people around feeling for their guns. He threw the document onto the table, put his hand on Ruby's shoulder, smiled and indicated for her to get up.

"Read and learn . . . cobbler. It is signed by your chief of operations here in Perth. See here . . . it is the seal of your director in Canberra, who has in turn been in touch with your legal department and our embassy. Ruby Peters is coming with me, now, unless you want me to escalate matters further."

As they turned to leave, a huge man blocked the door to their exit. He looked different and had attitude . . . and a mean face.

"And where do you think you're going pal . . . Geoff Norton, CIA Australasia. She is ours now. We lost one of our agents in your Heathrow Airport by her hand. Now it looks like she has covered her tracks by whacking your own agent, sent over to monitor her while she is in Australia. It is not the first time we have lost colleagues because of this trouble-maker.

She is coming back to the States to face the law . . . our law and that is that. There's also an outstanding felony charge concerning stolen diamonds."

Ruby was getting highly annoyed. They did not even address her directly in their arguing during the three-way fight for her custody. It had happened during other investigations. They completely ignored her. However, there was really nothing she could explain to improve the situation. It looked like K439 Pomphrey was no match for the ingenuity and strategy of these alliance collaborators. The matter of the diamonds had raised its ugly head yet again and Ruby could see the connection at once and where things were headed.

"It certainly was outstanding, seeing as you stole the diamonds from the Arabs before blowing up their bloody boat. I believe your agents lost another boat . . . no two boats and were defeated in the English Channel too, by Eric and me. You are just scumbags to kill two agents just to get to me," sneered Ruby.

Ruby's new analysis of the situation indicated that it was the CIAs intention all along, to kill the two young agents in order to capture her in a foreign country.

Ruby looked at Norton accusingly as he strode over to her, ready to grab her.

"You stupid bastards. You bloody crazy, meddling terrorists. What can I possibly have, that deserves you to take the lives of your Cathy and our Jack. You will pay for this. You killed them. It was you," shouted Ruby as she kicked the desk hard.

Pomphrey was thinking the same thing, and he knew of other interested parties that would kill Ruby too, before or after obtaining the information they wanted. He was nearly ready to set his own plan into action.

"Now look here you. You are under our custody now," shouted Norton back at her.

The man in the suit was listening through his earpiece. His facial expression changed to one of determination.

"No. She is under Australian custody now Norton and has the official documents of authority to leave with Pomphrey here," he shouted, raising his arm to stop Norton from grabbing Ruby by the neck.

Pomphrey had already started his programmed play, pressing his 'rescue' button, programmed to cause a sequence of actions, including sending his location to a Perth safe house.

"Very well then, I just need to have a quiet word with my client before we can leave," said Pomphrey briskly.

"Two minutes. That's all you get, before we take her into custody and fly her out to the States for questioning and charging. I am claiming her for the CIA as part of our agreement with Australia," answered Norton sharply, reaching for his communicator, ignoring the man in the suit.

Pomphrey moved Ruby to a corner of the room and held her arm tight as she struggled to attack Norton.

"We're going to be doing a runner Ruby. Get your skates on and wait for my mention of 'skate' and do not ask any questions or hesitate. Just run like hell and follow me . . . and activate your tracker in case you get yourself lost."

Suddenly, both Norton and the suited man received urgent messages, which affected operations under their direct control. Norton's message said that the American Embassy was under threat and an unoccupied van was reportedly parked at the front entrance. He ran out of the room without saying a word.

The suited man's message told him that he had to attend to a matter at the entrance to the airport . . . and that he was to hand Ruby over to Norton.

"Arthur, put Ruby in the lockup until I get back . . . oh, and have our Pomphrey here escorted out of the airport, ok? Put him in a secure Comm Car headed out to the zoo or some other public place, but far, far away from here. We'll sort out the legalities later of where Ruby should be detained."

Arthur nodded and proceeded to take the two of them out of the interview room. As they were passing by the exit from the security section, they noticed what appeared to be two Federal Police officers approaching quickly. Within seconds, they had deployed smoke grenades and tear gas, which landed near to Ruby and

Pomphrey. The men handed Pomphrey and Ruby some gas masks before running towards the exit, clearing a way forward, disabling gates and dealing with the few security agents who were still wondering what was going on.

"It's time to skate Ruby," shouted Pomphrey with a laugh.

They both ran to the perimeter of the airport as four more smoke grenades were set off, ensuring maximum confusion and public panic as loud wailing alarms sounded. Pomphrey pushed Ruby into a waiting police car, which took off immediately, sirens blaring and lights flashing. The driver said nothing.

"Where are you taking me? Who are you? You are not MI6 and definitely not ASIS or CIA. So, who are you and what do you want?" demanded Ruby.

Pomphrey smiled at her, a little out of breath but looking remarkably calm.

"Of course I'm not MI6 my dear. Only a crew of highly skilled, coordinated and trustworthy band of brethren could pull that little charade off . . . and we are mostly ex-military and intelligence anyway. We don't exercise enough though."

"Jacko's crew!" she shouted.

"More like an entire navy, actually. We were on to the CIAs plan as soon as they wasted their own agent at Heathrow. Of course, she was not an experienced agent at all. Cathy Summers was an aspiring actor that they found pounding the boards in Manchester, although she was born in California and did a bit of teaching there. Poor innocent girl . . . they promised her plenty, to carry out the secret agent role. However, our Jack Parton was the real deal, as you well know. Now I bet you did not know that Jack was in the SAS for five years – he served in Afghanistan and was badly wounded. They said he would be paralysed for life but got the nod from 'C' after he fully recovered. He would have done better with us instead. Such a brave lad. Very shy with women they say."

Ruby felt numb and did not react to his baiting. She was still on edge and needed to sleep. It had been thirty-six hours since she had a good sleep.

"I'm taking you to a safe house for a good feed, a warm bed and the opportunity to see how the intelligence service handles the media. They have to explain two major incidents at two international airports. Then you can decide what you want us to do. We do have some friendly contacts in the 'company' you know, mainly because we work together sometimes. We do the things that they are unable to do. So, we can be your neutral buffer while you are here with us."

"And is your real name Pomphrey? I mean, does anyone have a real name these days?" asked Ruby quietly.

"Pom Free. There you go . . . but it only works in Australia. Keep it like that or else everyone will get confused."

Ruby thought about Eric and his uncanny knack with anagrams and coded messages. His random logic and intuitive thinking would have seen through Pomphrey in an instant. It also brought her to thinking, that Davis must have left more information at his secret home in Brisbane or on the yacht in Hobart. Otherwise, why would everyone want to find her or kill her, unless to prevent the information from being revealed, she thought.

"I have to visit some places while I am here. I need to be free to do my own thing for a few weeks without anyone knowing. So if you don't mind, I'll leave after a couple of days and get lost in the void . . . do you understand?"

"That's fine Ruby. A bit like your Blackpool trip, I imagine. Again, I can offer our help wherever you are 24/7. I will let MI6 know what happened here and that you will be recovering for two weeks at destinations unknown . . . and that you are safe."

"Thank you for that. Do you think they will come looking for me?"

Pomphrey looked at her in amazement.

"You are a loose cannon Ruby, with potentially lethal information, given your reception so far. So yes, they and everyone else will be looking for you. You need to use all the skills you have learnt and a whole lot of good fortune. I can coordinate your return to the UK when you are ready. Just call me on this number . . . diverted phone of course. Are you financial . . . I mean . . . do you have access to cash?"

"Yes I am, and I'll call you when I'm ready. I can't thank you enough for saving me at the airport."

"Rather messy I feel, but most effective. I do not think 'C' will be very happy with the publicity though. Right then, let's get you into some digs for a couple of days. First of all, I must blindfold you until we get to our den. Is that ok?"

"Fine. You did save me and know about Jacko, so I have to trust you," answered Ruby.

"Well to make you feel better, I can quote you the safety deposit box that you accessed in Blackpool. It was . . . 234D. Only you have the PIN that went with it. Is that good enough?"

Ruby nodded and started to relax. She was safe amongst friends. Jacko was proving to be a most reliable partner.

They travelled about ten miles before pulling into an industrial estate with heavy locked gates and security cameras all around. Ruby expected to enter into one of the factory units but instead, a high-voltage switchyard building opened up, exposing a ramp down to a lower floor.

"Wow, this is impressive – just like the people who take over the world," exclaimed Ruby.

"Accountants? No, there are no accountants here."

Ruby looked at his straight-face expression before laughing. Pomphrey checked the time and turned on the radio to hear the latest news flash.

"After an incident at the Qantas boarding lounge in Heathrow Airport today, it has been confirmed that a young woman has died from an overdose of the drug Fentanyl. Police have informed us that this death has nothing to do with a security-training event, now unfolding at Perth

Airport, involving the simulated death of a passenger who was flying with Qantas. The Police Commissioner has said that the training exercise without prior public notice was to ensure that the public reacted as expected. The SAS based at Swanbourne and the tactical response team are working together on a new strategy to protect the airport in case of a terrorist assault. Just repeating . . . the Perth Airport has been used in a live demonstration for our security forces. There was a limited use of harmless smoke bombs and the sounding of airport alarms to create a real-time scenario, for handling passenger traffic and baggage lockdown. It lasted about fifteen minutes and was deemed to be a complete success. The Police Commissioner apologises for any worry or inconvenience that this may have caused to passengers."

Ruby could only think of poor Jack and his larrikin nature.

"We still don't know who killed Cathy and Jack. I didn't see anyone of interest around me. I should have picked up on something unusual . . . at least when I was leaving Jack. He was right behind me and there were only a few passengers remaining to exit the plane. Personally, I think it was the bloody CIA again. They don't care about life at all."

"Oh, I doubt that now Ruby, too risky and blatantly obvious, unless a third party got out of line, but at least our lads have retrieved his body. It will be sent back to England immediately for analysis. It looks to me, like he was 'spiked' with a nerve agent in the neck, otherwise he would have screamed out for assistance. Unfortunately, it only takes a few seconds to affect the brain, stop the heart and well, at least death is swift. We have video of everyone coming off your flight. We were allowed to have a copy because of Cathy's death in London. The police have been very cooperative. The bloody intelligence services only want to exclude us and put you away forever it seems. We will examine the last few passengers after you came through the exit door . . . unless they blended into the airport ground staff of course. Anyway, we will also have the video from London to compare both sets of passengers. Whoever is missing or was in the final ten passengers, will be our murderer."

Ruby thought for a moment like her Eric used to do.

"It could also have been one of those flirty flight attendants. Now that would have set Jack up to abandon all his training."

Perth Airport had become calm and boring again, in accordance with what the local security people would often say about their workplace. However, one room was a bit livelier.

"I'll have your bloody job for this you bloody morons. We had her secure, at the airport, ready for sending back to the States and you blew it. How the hell, did you manage not to see the activity of those smoke bombers . . . and as for that police car getaway, I mean you would not read about it! Where in the world did they get that gem? It looked like a throwback from the last century," screamed Norton.

The Australian security team were more than a little miffed at being reprimanded by a Yank, who had no authority over them at all. How such a young woman, barely out of spy school could be so important to them was beyond their imagination.

"Yeah, too bad mate, we were taken by surprise with the smoke and all. You should have warned us about the importance of this girl. I mean, what has she done? Geez, nothing like this has happened here before . . . anywhere, in Australia. Not until you American buggers came over here, with your bloody pommy problems. We ditched that lot years ago mate," replied the dark-suited man with a laugh before rethinking the situation."

He started fuming over the many things that had thwarted his own attempt to detain Ruby – such as who could be responsible for rescuing her, the identity of that snooty Pomphrey, with all the valid official papers and signatures . . . and the gall of Norton, just wandering into the airport central security office without being challenged sufficiently. His size and anger had a lot to do with that.

Norton was about to storm out of the room when the door opened violently, to the surprise of the dark-suited man.

"Major Caldwell! I was not expecting you in person. I thought you were in Canberra."

"Not much you do know is there Baker, and who's this interloper in our top security area?" shouted Caldwell, glaring at Norton.

"This is . . ."

"Major Norton, Geoff Norton, CIA, on special assignment to take Ruby Peters into custody and fly her back to the States. She's wanted for various felonies, accessory to murder, grand theft . . . I could go on," interrupted Norton with his stretched out hand.

The Major turned away without shaking his hand, speaking directly to Baker and raising his voice.

"Get him out of here immediately . . . after checking his ID and his person thoroughly. Then I want a full rundown on why our airport was smoke bombed, why the airport was not on high alert . . . and why hundreds of distressed passengers have appeared on TVs around the world, crying and screaming. This is bloody Perth man . . . not bloody Iraq."

"Yes sir, Major, I'll get right on it. Arthur, Josh. Take Major Norton here to the examination room and give him the full run down. Then escort him out of the airport."

"Now look here, you bloody colonial bunch of . . ." started Norton.

"Make it a very thorough examination Arthur. I have no record of him obtaining a high-level pass to enter our security area. You think you own us . . . well not on my watch Chuck," interrupted Caldwell with a scowl.

Norton went screaming and shouting out of the room with Arthur and Josh, threatening to escalate the situation up to military level.

"If you don't keep quiet, I'll have to handcuff you and put you in solitary. Understand Norton . . . mate?" whispered Arthur.

"Bloody Yanks," added Josh shaking his head.

Back in the office, Major Caldwell was answering a phone call put through to him.

"Ah Major, this is Reginald Masterson, the British consular service in Perth. I believe you have one of our citizens in custody at the Perth airport . . . a Ruby Peters. If you would be so kind as to let me know the facts of the matter, then I am sure that we can make . . . certain diplomatic arrangements and get her out of your way. You know she is MI6 don't you Major? Nothing grand, just administration you know, but she does have certain rights between our two countries. We are still on the same side, barring the cricket and rugby."

Caldwell was fuming.

"Did you not send someone by the name of Pomphrey to us, in the last hour?"

"Pomphrey? Never heard of anyone by that name. My goodness, I hope you didn't let her go with that chap, Major. It is bad enough to lose an agent on one of your planes . . . but an ongoing problem with a kidnapped agent is highly problematical."

"She escaped in the mayhem that was caused by a rescue attempt. I assumed that your lot would not do such a thing Masterson, not with the smoke bombs and violence in a public place . . . and in a sovereign country. So I am wondering, just who would be brazen enough to storm the airport and take her with them. Apparently, it was quite a voluntary kidnapping too. It looks like you have the problem there Masterson. We still have to deal with a sizeable clean-up bill and a PR nightmare to sort out. Of course, we are saying that it was specialised training and all that, in the media announcements. We don't want to look like fools."

"Quite . . . no you can't have that perception, Major."

Masterson already knew that the 'company' had used 'mercenary help' in extracting Ruby from the clutches of the CIA. They had no option but to rely on Jacko's crew, due to the almost certain use of limited force and with the rescue being in such a public place.

The UK Home Office was extremely upset at the loss of one of their younger agents. They had duly informed the Prime Minister who was now in close contact with the American Presidential office. Reading between the lines at the PMs diplomatic 'questioning', the President had told the CIA not to aggravate the tense situation, although he fully expected them to continue to look for Ruby.

Back at Vauxhall cross, 'C' was in a follow-up meeting with the PM to discuss what to do about Ruby.

> "We need to get her back here as soon as possible and interrogate her . . . formally. We have found out through GCHQ that the information she has or may not even know she has yet, will be extremely damaging for many nations. Then of course, there is the potential terrorist threat that could arise if they get hold of that information and use it to their advantage," said 'C' sternly to his security cabinet.

> "What is it . . . this information she may or may not have? I thought she was working with us. I mean she is on the books so to speak as a Grade 3 FIO," asked the Prime Minister cautiously.

All eyes turned to 'C', who looked over to the anxious Defence Force Chief.

> "She is 100 per cent on the team PM. I will guarantee you that. The information we are talking about may contain the whereabouts of planted, ready to go, dirty bombs, placed in various locations by a terrorist group quite a few years ago, in order to blackmail a country into giving them 'certain privileges'," replied 'C'.

> "And where are these bombs located? Are they in the UK? What are we doing about it? We are talking nuclear devices aren't we? Are they here in London?" hurried the Prime Minister.

> "Yes PM, they are dormant nuclear devices. Davidson here is our chief intelligence analyst at GCHQ. Tell them. Tell our members where they are supposedly located," said 'C' with a sigh.

> "London, Paris, New York, Moscow . . . Beijing, Berlin . . . Hong Kong . . ."

"Thank you Davidson. That is enough for the moment. We do not want to scare everyone at this early stage. Keep in touch . . . and keep your disposal teams ready for a quick and full response," ushered 'C', waving him away.

"So where is she? Where is our Ruby?" asked the Prime Minister.

"We did have her PM until the bloody CIA bullied their way into the Australian security enclosure. As you know, we were forced to use a third party to secure her from the Americans. It is all in my report. Rather messy approach . . . but deemed necessary at the time. The media has been placated by the Australians. They have been very cooperative considering it all happened on their national carrier. All we have to do now is coordinate her return . . . but apparently, she has had other ideas and has absconded from their care. I think she has a damn good idea where the information could be located and like us when we were in lock down a few years back . . . she will not trust anyone else. We knew Davis used to travel to Australia, which is why we sent Ruby there. She was not part of my original 'meet and greet' team . . . not with her, shall we say . . . attitude to the Americans. We are sending more people over there now but it could be a bloody battle to get to her first. I have the utmost confidence in our Ruby, PM."

The Prime Minister shook his head wearily and left the room, following the directions of Davidson. 'C' turned towards his closest and most trusted agent.

"Tian, I want you over there to bring her back . . . before anyone else finds her and those damn newspapers get in the way. I am quite sure that Davis would have deposited any secret papers somewhere whilst in Australia. We know he went there off and on, but we do not know where exactly. You knew him Tian. What do you think?"

"Yes, I totally agree sir. Roger was the type to invent many false trails and in Australia anyone can lose themselves in the cities, in a crowd or the even in the bush. He always loved to impersonate others and create fictitious characters. He could fit in anywhere."

'C' was aware of some of the wild characters that Davis used to play, sometimes tricking his colleagues with ad lib performances, to test them out . . . and their patience.

"And Ruby? Would he really trust a young girl like that, with such important information," quizzed 'C'.

"She was an innocent sir . . . not aligned or against anybody. I think he treated her like no other person in his life. Maybe it was even love . . . regret or maybe she was the daughter he never had. Who knows, but she is definitely the one he would have trusted . . . and wanted to make good with her, after that disastrous recruiting debacle."

"I see. Well then, the next question is . . . where would Roger Davis have constructed his foxhole? Where did he travel and what did he do when he was there? Check all that Tian, before you go. Holiday photos, people he spoke with, credit cards, health records, real estate and taxation files, favourite food . . . wine - anything that will give us a clue as to where he went. Just bring Ruby back . . . alive and with any information she has found, before someone else gets to her," continued 'C'.

Tian looked him in the eye and nodded.

"I've worked with Davis on a few occasions and like everyone else regarded him as the best. He was thorough and had an eye for detail, although his deep thinking and lone behaviour made him seem rather boring . . . except for his occasional funny antics when he'd had a few drinks Then with Ruby . . . well I thought I knew Ruby very well, up until she took that one day off, concealing all traces of her movements. That was quite an act. She has been trained well, even though I did have to save her a few times in the early days. She is street smart and has a strong moral ethic. I think Ruby will be very safe until I find her. I should be looking for a trail of people who have sore legs."

'C' smiled and put his hand on her shoulder.

"Even I keep well away from her when reprimanding her.

Have a good flight and keep in touch with me directly. Do not go through any other channel, unless you use the location router. This is too serious a matter, to be ruined by a determined hacker. Your plane leaves in two hours from Heathrow . . . better get a move on."

Identity

R uby woke up late the next morning. After eight hours of restful sleep, she felt refreshed but a little light headed. The thought crossed her mind that her nightcap may have been 'doctored' to ease her emotional pain. She took a moment to remember the cheeky Jack Parton, sent to protect her on QF9 after Cathy Summers murder at Heathrow. She knew he meant well and was putting on a bit of a show to hide his true nature. He was now sadly, another statistic, uniquely intertwined within her own difficult life. She was just starting to like his casual adventurous ways and his concealed interest in her. It was time for her to go.

She raced into the main room and asked Ben Sandford to download the contents from her lapel camera. It had been recording during the interview at the airport.

"Now we'll see who our friends at ASIS and CIA really are and get to the bottom of all this nonsense. Someone has to pay for killing two agents . . . and for poor Jack. Someone will pay for this," she murmured to herself.

"Now Ruby, don't let past events cloud your judgement. If you are going to be away from us for a while, you will need to be fully alert. Concentrate on the present moment. I am so very sorry about Jack. He seemed so . . ." replied Sanford who had overheard her mutterings.

"Young, Ben . . . so young and full of life. Just like my Eric was . . . and always will be . . . 'Forever Young'."

Ben Sandford smiled softly and touched her arm as he left her to work. He hesitated, turned around and produced a package wrapped up in bubble-wrap.

"Here Ruby, take this with you. You may need it as a last resort . . . but keep it well hidden. They are illegal here and you are not covered by MI6 to use any weapon whilst in Australia."

"What is it?" asked Ruby, surprised.

"A Beretta Bobcat 22 . . . the Russkies like them . . . Da? It distinguishes you from the Federal police and their Glocks, should you fire it in public. In case you don't know, they are a .40 Smith and Wesson version of the full-sized Glock 17, introduced in the nineties. Pomphrey will get you a wad of cash by the way. You will need quite a bit for just one week of travel, accommodation and incidentals. You can pay the money back from your own bank later, to one that Jacko uses for . . . 'heavy lifting' We can also give you a motorbike but we want it back in one piece. Look after it, ok?"

"Great thanks. I have nearly finished here. Didn't find much. Except Norwood from the CIA was part of the investigation into that diamond theft. It involved two agents killed in England at the same place as Roger Davis. They were mixed up with the Arabs in money laundering for another project . . . most likely illegal too."

"Probably one of many deals outside of their license. My old mate Davis eh? . . . Now he was a top bloke and a terrific field agent, so meticulous and careful. I was surprised to hear that he was ambushed on a quiet country road in England . . . not like him at all. He used that same motorbike over there a few times you know . . . pumped up a few miles on it alright. Yeah, I reckon he headed over east to Melbourne or maybe Sydney. Do you know where you are headed first Ruby? This is your first trip to the land of Oz isn't it?"

Ruby thought quickly.

"I will be travelling light and fast . . . and I'm sorry, I can't say."

Sandford laughed and walked away again.

"It was worth a try. Don't forget to eat. Try the Hungry Jacks burgers Ruby. That will keep you going. Davis always liked the 'bacon deluxe burger' . . . but I digress. Keep safe and well Ruby."

Ruby's mind was still ticking over from the events leading up to Davis's death and the uncovering of the four 'moles' within MI6. Many agencies and groups had wanted that information, now all in the past and settled . . . but maybe there was more . . . and she had not found it in his safe deposit box. She was thinking that whatever he tucked away from the prying eyes of his own people must be related to an international field assignment.

Pomphrey entered the room carrying two cups of coffee.

"I hope you slept well and getting back on track Ruby. Here, this should shake the cobwebs out of you."

"Thank you. Yes I slept almost too well, if you know what I mean. I needed the rest."

Pomphrey smiled with raised eyebrows and produced a packet of original Tim Tams.

"Here, don't eat them all at once. What are you looking for Ruby . . . anything in particular?" he asked quizzically.

He could see that Ruby had just typed in the name of the sociopath who murdered her Eric. The file on Feliks Bielski and his mother Kata, showed the disastrous link between their betrayal to the Russians and an unknown MI6 informant . . . along with some of Davis's notes.

"I am trying to find a link between the people who want to kill me and all that has happened over the last ten years. Davis was the agent assigned to provide the Bielski's in Poland with a safe passage to England, in return for the list of 'moles' she had obtained from the Russians. Kata had met a gruesome death after being severely tortured and her son Feliks was also tortured and had developed severe mental problems. Davis survived, bringing the list of 'moles' back to England, engraving the information in code, on to one of my reward diamonds . . . the same diamond that my Eric decoded. There is nothing further to suggest that Davis hid anything else from that assignment. There must be something else."

"I agree with you there. From what I have learnt talking with Jacko over the years, Davis was on to something so big, that he was a changed man . . . driven, deep and moody. Would not talk about it to anyone. Not the best of places to be in when your life is on the line every waking moment. Anyway, you may like to know that I am supposed to send you back to MI6 immediately, probably for an interrogation . . . but I will tell them that you have escaped.

I . . . we think that you may happen to stumble on what Davis was so worried about. All we ask is that you come back to us first, so that we can help you to decide what to do with the information. We do have a mutual trust now, I think. 'C' will go off his brain of course and eventually we will pass on the information but only when we think it is safe to do so. He is very keen to tidy this mess up as soon as possible."

"Wow! Interrogate me, one of their own and not quite two months into the job? Blimey, I think they've got a nerve," shouted Ruby.

Pomphrey looked sad and serious as he spoke.

"I would not want to be in your shoes at this time because you are in great danger and they will hunt you down mercilessly, until you reveal what Davis has hidden . . . or until you are no longer of any use . . . reached your expiry date. Look, we will take you away from here and drop you off in a suitable public place where there are no cameras. Here is a pile of cash for you by the way.

Do not take the motorbike! It would probably be the worst thing you could do. Be ready in five minutes and I will get you away myself. Sounds silly coming from me . . . but do not trust anybody. I would offer you our complete resources, but that would only make you stand out more . . . too many cooks. You never know who has turned anymore. There is no loyalty or respect anymore."

Pomphrey left the room as Ruby prepared her getaway rucksack complete with clothes, cash and gun. She looked at the rucksack and then at her reflection in the mirror. She looked different somehow to what she expected.

"You will wake up one day, Ruby Peters," she whispered to herself.

Ruby thought about the first time she met Davis and the day he offered her a lift to school with Eric and was mistakenly identified by an Arab consortium as someone of 'value'. Scarab, their leader, kidnapped Ruby believing he could get a ransom from Davis in the form of secret information about a new military site. Her Eric had reached out and saved her and through his actions had won her heart. All this brought her thoughts back to the stolen cache of diamonds and the rogue CIA agents who had died trying to get them back. It was then, that Ruby realised that the recent events were not really about her after all.

It was only the information they wanted, the hidden, mysterious notes made by a frightened man who could trust no one – and she was the only person who knew the location of his foxholes.

Some people would do anything to get at her, to tear her apart, looking for that secret cache. She expected that they would not force it out of her, as they may need her for deciphering any Davis code that was to expected. It would be another of his safeguards.

Ruby intended to visit two places – Brisbane where Davis had given her his house, car and bank accounts, and then Hobart, to see his boat moored in a marina – now her boat.

She half-expected more clues hidden at these sites, such as keys or passwords or codes, to open up the final resting place of any highly secret information. If it did exist, Ruby expected that it must be of a most dangerous kind. For Roger Davis not to have disclosed it to the 'company' or even Jacko's crew, it would indeed have to be 'enormous'.

> "Come on Ruby, it's time to go. You need a good head start. Just remember, like I said, this information must be so terrifying . . . that even poor Roger didn't know what the hell to do with it. Watch your back. Trust nobody, do you here?" cautioned Pomphrey.

> "I'm ready. Thank you for helping me. I won't let you down . . . and I do want to go home."

Ruby thought that Pomphrey was a bit too keen to see her on her way. She knew that her clothing and rucksack would need to be dumped yet again, and new ones bought for cash. Even the money needed to be checked for any 'devices' or dyes that could potentially track her somehow. It was becoming the norm.

She still felt that Roger Davis was somehow guiding her towards what he had intended to do with the rest of his life. For now, it was up to her to be the agent and confidante he had nurtured and protected. It was time to test her skills and cunning to the limit.

The Plan

Pomphrey dropped Ruby off at the Swan Bell Tower near the Elizabeth Quay, just as 'the bells' were playing on the hour. To fill in some time and check out if anyone was following her, she boarded the small ferry to South Perth, located on the other side of the Swan River. She took with her a brochure about the Indian Pacific train. It was leaving for Sydney the next day.

The train station, at the boundary of Northbridge and the city, also has a discount-shopping precinct, ideal for dumping her gear and for buying new clothes and another rucksack.

It was still early morning but already the temperature had climbed to thirty degrees Centigrade. It was a sticky reminder that the seasons were opposite to England, where the cold, damp winter did not seem too extreme after all. She walked up to what looked like an information centre.

"Excuse me. Can you tell me if it is better to go by road or train across the Nullarbor? I'm new to Australia and I want a fast, safe trip over to Sydney," she asked the bright young woman at the tourist kiosk.

"Hello. Sure, I can help you with that. The train gets to Sydney within two days and you can relax, dine, sleep and just chill out. It is a bit expensive though. You're looking at around two thousand dollars . . . each way."

"Wow, that's heaps for a train ride!"

"Yes, but then you are travelling about five thousand kilometres in comfort and complete safety. The road trip is the opposite – long and dangerous, with kangaroos and emus, and even camels in the middle of the road. You certainly would not want to drive at night and hit one of those buggers. Most people except the truckies stop driving when it gets to dusk . . . and then there is the long distance between fuel, water, accommodation . . ." she continued, waving her hand from side to side like a rag doll.

"Wow, I get it. I would need a car as well, so I would have to rent something suitable. Maybe a tank," interrupted Ruby.

"You can always hire a campervan . . . but it's the same thing with the night animals, and if you're going solo . . . well I would not want to be stuck out there on my own. Have you thought about . . . flying? You would be there in four hours."

Ruby put on her sunglasses as she thought about going back to Perth Airport, prompting her to check out her surroundings, for signs of company. Flying from Perth was not an option.

"I get airsick but thanks for your advice. I will take the train and eat baked beans for the rest of my holidays. I love your top by the way," said Ruby waving, before eyeing up a colourful sign for the Perth Zoo.

"It's just down the road, a few hundred metres away," shouted the lady, "Some of the animals may be taking a snooze in this heat though. Half their luck. Bye."

Ruby walked along the road and down a slight incline to the Zoo entrance to pay her entry fee. Then she headed straight for the toilets after looking around cautiously again, almost automatically. She thought that if she were going to die, it would not be sitting on a public toilet.

After a quick change of top, a revamp to her hair into a style that fitted inside her cap and covering her rucksack with a green t-shirt, she checked her belongings using Eric's small 'bug' detector. 'Beep, Beep, Beep' just as she thought. The rucksack and her coat had miniature aerials that activated detectors, powered by an external source. Once removed, she made them readily available for dumping. She guessed that the clothes may be marked for item recognition on the cameras, so they would still need to be changed.

The nearest animal enclosure to the toilets was the baboons, surrounded by children most unsure of the look of their raw bottoms. A quick flick of the hand despatched one of the tracking devices into the back of a passing tourist train. It was just leaving for a circumnavigation of the entire zoo.

Ruby used the phone that Pomphrey had given her, to book a seat on the train using her 'company' credit card. Although she had purchased a new SIM card, Ruby knew that the phone was tracking her every move, but it would save her a heap of cash for just one diversionary phone call. Once booked, the phone disappeared deep inside a full feed-bin, marked 'Orang-utan'. One of their toys was sitting to the side . . . a good depository for the second tracking device.

"They won't like me making a monkey out of them again," giggled Ruby as the zookeeper waved at her with a smile.

Ruby screwed her nose up with delight as she headed back outside, hidden within a group of European tourists with noisy laughing children. They seemed to enjoy Ruby's close proximity as she laughed along with them, making funny animal faces.

Across the road was a taxi rank with four cabs containing four weary, heat-stressed drivers. She ran across the road and got in the front cab.

"Hello. Can you please take me to the shopping mall called 'Watertown' . . . I think it is in West Perth. Is that right?"

"Oh, yes very good. I think it is there too . . . then that makes for a most pleasant ride Miss, when we are both thinking the same way. It is nice shopping there for sure. Maybe a bit expensive . . . but there is a lot of choice," replied the driver with a thick Indian accent and a wide smile.

Ruby reached into her bag to get some cash for the trip, spilling out a few hundred dollars onto her lap.

"Oh, I think you will be very happy there Miss. You can spend all day in there and come away with everything you will ever need," laughed the driver.

"Yes, I'm sorry. I have just been to the ATM and this has to last me for two weeks," replied Ruby quickly.

He looked her up and down with exaggeration and a very wide smile, nodding his head approvingly.

"Oh my goodness. I am so very lucky to have a super model in my taxi today. My friends will not believe me when I tell them so. It is indeed my lucky day today . . . very, very lucky indeed."

Ruby looked at the expressive driver and then at his official looking portrait on his ID, to make sure he was actually the driver. There was an indication that this man knew how to play his business.

> "Well . . . Dinesh . . . I think that deserves some reward in itself. I know it's only a short ride across the Narrows Bridge, but I'll see you right for being so charming . . . and honest."

Dinesh flashed his wide smile again, looking like he was the king of the road because she had taken the trouble to find out his name. When they arrived at the centre, Ruby realised that she only had one hundred-dollar notes and that it would be difficult for the driver to give her change for only a ten-dollar ride – something not unnoticed by the ever beaming Dinesh.

> "Hmmm. If I ever come back this way again Dinesh, I hope to see you again with the sole aim of going into business with you. Here . . . it is indeed your lucky day. Thank you for the ride. Bye."

> "You are most welcome anytime to ride in my wonderful taxi Miss. Anytime at all. I can wait if you want. You are so very kind and also . . ."

> "That's your lot Dinesh. I walk from here, ok?" quipped Ruby with a grin and a wave.

Ruby quickly did her round of the shopping precinct, choosing summery, but not 'stand-out' clothing for her long trip. She changed the rucksack for a simple grey-green one, leaving the old one for the eager young salesman, at the shop counter. He had helped her to try it on – which is what Ruby was thinking in a different way.

The next step was to find somewhere to stay overnight before catching the train . . . or not. She had now formulated each component of a well thought out plan. Confident that no one was following, Ruby left the shops and headed for a small house not far away. It was 4pm and it was much hotter than at noon. The shops had been a welcome respite from the heat, but even the short walk had been quite unpleasant for her. She was exhausted through not drinking enough and her face was red and blotchy.

'Walton House' looked like the website brochure, all except for the dirty surroundings, with old-style factory units and shops that had seen better days. The proximity to the city was there but not the 'leafy inner suburb elegance', a 'stone's throw' from all transport and 'five-star' restaurants. She had seen a rough looking pizza shop and a dirty looking café approaching the hotel.

Ruby sauntered up to the foyer to check-in.

"Hello there. Sam Mowbray . . . checking in for the night and a good rest," she said with a sigh.

"Hi there, I'm Robbie the owner . . . well part owner with my wife of course. Bec's away getting in some supplies. Just the one nighter is it then Sam? Ah yes, I see you on here," replied the middle-aged man with a calming voice.

"Yes, just the one night this time around. I will probably book another night or two for when I come back to Perth in a few weeks."

"Good, that sounds like a plan to me. You are in room 14, up the stairs and to the right. We have snacks and drinks available from the office from 7am until 8pm every day and then dinner is in our dining room from 7pm. There's no room service . . . but of course every room has its own facilities . . . bathroom, TV, microwave oven, electric jug and a fridge packed with what I call . . . comfort foods, and relaxing beverages," he raced through, in what seemed like one breath.

"Wow, that all sounds good to me. Do you mind if I pay with cash, either now or in the morning, only I am not a fan of all this credit business? I tend to spend too much and I lost my card once. What a stressful time that was."

"I understand. Anyway, cash is king, so they say Sam. If you can pay two hundred dollars now . . . and then we will pay you back in the morning, for whatever is left, should you use anything in your fridge. I have a feeling that the drinks will disappear as soon as you get in your unit. You do look hot . . . I mean, you know, temperature wise," he blurted out embarrassingly, "The actual rate here is one hundred and fifty per night. Is that OK? I will give you a receipt each time."

"Yes, that's fine. Thank you. I'll pay you now," replied Ruby looking away at the brochure display.

As soon as she was in her room, Ruby took out the rather thin looking chicken sandwiches and a warm orange juice that she had purchased at the shopping centre. She checked out the fridge, staring lovingly at the ice-cold beers, white wine and the marvellous collection of chocolate, fudges and potato chips. In went the sandwiches and orange juice - out came a Carlsberg and her very own Cadbury buffet.

After turning on the TV, she settled back with some more chocolate and a coffee. After swirling it around in her mouth slowly, she fell onto the bed with a bag of potato chips, to watch the in-house movie that was due to begin. When it was only half way through, she decided to take a long hot shower and have an early night. She had experienced a rare luxury – peace and relaxation from her worries . . . and ready to fight another day.

Illusion

Ruby was already out of bed by 7am, munching on one of her now dried-up chicken sandwiches while swirling huge chunks of fudge in her mouth with a hot coffee. She knew that anyone looking for her would be checking one of a number of departure points: the airport; the bus depot; the train station; hire car and camper rentals and used car yards.

The 'company' would be very angry and worried that she had 'escaped' Jacko's Australian rescue team, divesting herself of all their tracking devices. She imagined that the accountants at MI6 would never give up with their audit trail of her expenses.

However, by evading her own people, other interested parties were now on the same level playing field and may even have an advantage.

Ruby sat on the bed and closed her eyes, taking a few minutes 'time-out' to meditate over her day's plan, seeing herself acting out each part to see if it was workable. As she opened her eyes wide, her plan had become clear. It was to work outside of the box because everyone would expect her to use her skills by the book. Her aim was not to act like a resourceful field agent with specialised training at all. In fact she would play 'mix and match' with different strategies to disrupt any sense of logical form. Ruby was certain that Tian would be pleased with her plan. Her Tao philosophy of being formless and 'keeping the externals at bay' had certainly kept her alive through the years.

After paying the hotel bill with an extra forty dollars for her fridge frivolity, Ruby ventured outside, carefully looking up and down the street. She walked around the corner into a supermarket car park, checking out the layout and as expected, there was a taxi bay outside the main entrance. There were three cabs on the rank.

She walked past the first two until she spotted the third driver fast asleep, sunglasses on, and Indian music wafting over his smiling face. She got in the front and closed the door quietly.

"This is your lucky day indeed Dinesh . . . and to think that out of all the cabs in Perth, you would be here waiting for me . . . just as you suggested . . . almost, as if you knew what I was thinking," she said quietly.

"Oh my goodness, young lady. You have been surprising me and I am being asleep . . . or maybe still dreaming . . . it is so nice to see you again . . . Oh, yes it is. You have come to ride in my wonderful taxi again. I am a very, very lucky . . ." he gushed, before Ruby interrupted.

"Dinesh . . . I have a big problem. I want to travel to Adelaide and need to know where I can . . . hitch a ride . . . to get me there, without anyone seeing me. You see I have overstayed my travel visa and if I go by bus, train, plane or hire-car, they will find me and I will go to prison. I was thinking about a long distance truck . . . but I want to be safe. Do you know of anything?"

Dinesh was astonished at her predicament and his face showed it. He looked rather alarmed that he was now in a difficult situation.

"I'm sorry Dinesh. Maybe I should not have asked you this. Just take me to the train station. I will risk it and trust in fate. Prison can't be all that bad . . . I suppose."

"No, no . . . let me think Miss. Oh, you are in a very bad situation and I know a little about . . . these visas. Some of my friends . . . well, their friends, have been here maybe too long and they also tell me to take them to places. Now I am thinking I can know a better way Miss . . . and I can help you as I must, for indeed you are a true friend. I can tell these things for sure. You have been too generous already to me and my family."

"What do you think then Dinesh? My name is Sam by the way."

"Oh what a wonderful name. It is truly a very lucky name. Well now Sam, I think you should drive to Geraldton and then catch a plane from there to go to Adelaide. This will be most unexpected and you will not be noticed in there, flying from a country airport. They are very easy going and just want to go home. But you must change how you look. Oh you will still look very nice I am sure . . . but truly different," he replied quietly.

Ruby looked at his honest face and then at his photo ID again. She doubted whether he had ever come across an MI6 spy who could deliver a leg-breaking kick and packed a Beretta Bobcat as hand luggage.

"And how do I get to Geraldton? How far is it Dinesh?"

"It is about four hundred kilometres and about . . . oh, a four-hour drive from Perth. Miss Sam . . . I could take you there in my beautiful clean cab for just a small fee . . . I will let you decide how much. You are a very honest young lady. Did I not say that you are a super model and have a wonderful . . .?"

Ruby looked at him quizzically as he carried on with his excited realisation that today was a very, very lucky day.

"How does one thousand dollars sound Dinesh? Would that cover all your expenses? I can pay upfront but I need to know that you will do it safely . . . and basically . . . right now."

Dinesh could not contain himself and quoted verses of scriptures and wisdom that Ruby worked out to be a firm 'Yes'.

The long trip was a mixture of beautiful Indian music and lively talk about his home in India with his wife and two children, before they emigrated for a better life in Australia. It didn't take long for Dinesh to lose his stereotype banter. It was like watching Davis do his thing.

Ruby told him a modified life story of how she would have wanted to live - with her Eric and a life of peace and quiet in the English countryside, close to her parents. This made Dinesh homesick, and for all his travels, he found he could not fit in with this strange new culture. The old ways were deeply entrenched in his mind, even though he did not openly show it. His children absolutely loved their new country and the bonus of having Indian friends in a close community made Dinesh accept the fact that he was better off here in many ways. He was also self-employed.

They stopped off for food and drinks along the way and a chance to stretch their legs. The funny side was that they were travelling through the country in a Perth taxi, which everyone seemed to stare and point out. However, the people hunting down Ruby would not have expected such a novel and bold plan of action.

Just before Geraldton, Ruby called into a pharmacy for some toiletries, finding out from the staff that one of the motels nearby had plenty of rooms available. The school holidays had just finished.

After saying goodbye to Dinesh and wishing him a safe trip back to Perth, she paid the motel for the night upfront in cash and quickly closed her door. The area looked a little rough and there were people hanging around outside the tavern next door.

The next few hours transformed Ruby into a different person – looser hair with a fringe, the colour a few tones lower and with different makeup. Rummaging through her bag, she produced a floppy cap that fell low over her face. A pair of plain coloured glasses completed the look.

Next, she used one of the credit cards that had been in Davis's safety deposit box, to pay the airline using the motel phone. This time she was travelling under one of her new names, Sandra Jacobs, one of several that Davis had prepared for her along with ample banking facilities.

She called for an Uber to take her to the airport, paying with the same credit card. It was a far better proposition than paying by cash – which attracted attention for different reasons when used for a big-ticket item, especially a flight.

At the airport, she kept her face low, into a book, from the time she arrived until the plane took off. The security had been a breeze to get through, with the staff actually smiling and not looking at anything except their cramped work area. Ruby thought that this was due to them being in a country town, far away from the pressures of city security concerns.

After saying a quick hello to her fellow passenger, a man in jeans with a 'high-visibility' shirt, she checked her surroundings, then pretended to fall asleep listening to the on-board radio.

The man had a few beers at the start of the flight before fiddling around on his i-pad once the plane was at full altitude. He looked a little shy and unsure whether he should speak to her. For Ruby, this was the ideal situation, as she could now listen to the radio and not turn around again until the plane was landing.

Adelaide airport seemed very spacious to her but unusually quiet for a major airport. She kept her head down, standing away from where the cameras would be located, quickly checking for the exit once she had retrieved her rucksack from baggage collection.

It was obvious that there were quite a few undercover security personnel looking at the passengers and checking out any suspicious activity. However, Ruby remained calm and contained within her new persona, moving slowly with head down looking at her mobile phone screen, pretending to be with other people. The face detection software would be checking for a match up to any persons of interest. Whether it was up and running was another matter. She also wondered if they could detect the false nose padding . . . or her eyes behind those stretched-out glasses.

"Hey there! Wait! Stop!" boomed a voice behind her, before feeling a firm hand restraining her shoulder.

Ruby froze and turned around slowly, to see a huge man with wide shoulders thrusting something towards her. She had no time to react. She waited for a knife to cut her down.

"You dropped this just now," he said with a quiet voice, offering it to her, looking strangely at the nose-padding half-hanging down her cheek.

"Oh, yes, thank you, my magazine. I forgot that I was carrying that. Thank you. I was in a bit of a tizzy with this allergic runny nose of mine," replied Ruby with what seemed to the trained eye, to be a look of sheer relief.

Ruby ran across to the first available taxi and sat in the back, quickly sorting out her disintegrating face.

"Hi, can you take me to the Britz campervan rental offices please."

The driver drove off straight away without looking at her. He did not say anything during the ride either until getting close to the destination. The radio was on low, full of advertising and talk-over, and little music.

> "Britz wasn't it?" he shouted, peering in the rear vision mirror at his fare who was staring at his ID card.

> "Yes Britz. What do I owe you then?"

> "Make it thirty dollars even. Want a receipt?"

> "Here's thirty five cash. No receipt thanks. Oh, and can you drive me around the block . . . I want to surprise my boyfriend. He is not expecting me."

The driver sighed and continued driving. After stopping, he reached out to take the money and caught her eye again before turning back to quickly reset his meter back to 'day shift'. He waited until she got out before driving off again. Ruby wondered about his life, meeting so many people each day without connecting or overthinking his life. At least he had a private life, yet paradoxically was always on public show, she thought.

There was a wide variety of campervans on display in the parking lot. Reaching for the next 'shifter-produced' passport in her collection, Ruby walked briskly towards the office, as a young man wearing corporate blazer and a warm smile approached her at equal speed.

> "Hello there. How may I help you today? My name is David. Are you looking for a camper?" he asked, immediately regretting the obvious.

> "Hello, I am Alice . . . Palmer. Yes, I would like a campervan for three days, to travel to Brisbane, one way, for my boyfriend and me. We are on holidays from England. He is off buying some provisions so I will pay for the lot. Do you take American Express?"

> "No worries Alice. We take anything including cash, credit cards and bank transfers . . . but none of that 'bit coin' shit," he laughed, "So you can have that one over there for ninety dollars per day. It is easy to drive and has superb air-conditioning. You will need that for sure, going up to 'Brizzy' in summer. I can sign you up if you would like to come up to the office. You are probably looking at four hundred dollars

all up, with insurance. So, I'll need your international driver's licence and passport, and the Amex card too."

Ruby handed over the documents and Amex card from the bundle of new identities and financial documents she was carrying. She had previously checked the online accounts to know that there was at least two hundred thousand dollars in the various bank balances she was accessing, courtesy of Davis.

"Do you have your boyfriend's passport and driving licence handy? I presume he'll be driving the vehicle too."

Ruby had not thought that far ahead. Rummaging through her bag again, she found the documents intended for her Eric. His papers were all in the name of 'Damon Spiers'. She dared not look at his photo.

"Here you are," replied Ruby, "his nickname is 'Diamond' on account of his first name."

"Rough or polished Alice? Sorry, that's not very funny."

"Oh, he's more like a rolling stone I'm afraid," laughed Ruby.

After signing the papers and an overly extended tour of the campervan, Ruby said good-bye to David, who followed her out, eagerly helping her to climb up into the van. He felt the warmth of her hand as they shared a passing glance. Ruby would have loved to have stayed longer, to get to know him better. She gave him a warm smile. David knew he would not forget this lithe English girl with a warmth and depth not generally seen in his circle of friends.

She started the engine and settled back to commence her trip. David looked on with a sigh. He imagined that she had just mouthed the words 'Good-bye', but he was still transfixed within a thoughtful moment in time.

Ruby checked her side mirror and smiled again softly. Chance, time and reality had defeated her once more.

Many Players

As Ruby travelled on the road to Brisbane to assess the assets gifted to her by Davis, there were many people searching for her in the blistering Australian summer heat. Her last known position was Perth and she had already survived two attempts on her life. It was hot and muggy and working out the intricacies of the air conditioner settings was her first priority.

However, back in London, it was cold and wet. 'C' was keeping an eye on the developments from his home. He was worried about Ruby going it alone. The Defence Chief was on standby for immediate deployment of military weapon specialists and military aircraft. His wife Jenny had never seen him so concerned about his work, as he sat quietly at the table watching Melissa and Toby play with their food. He wondered what sort of a world he would pass on if he got things wrong.

Jenny knew well not to ask about his work, but this time seemed different. As he felt her concerns, he looked towards her and smiled softly, thinking about the time they met and the time when they nearly called it quits . . . because of his consuming work.

> "What are you thinking about Reggie? I have never asked you before but . . . I think you need to talk to me this time, about what is worrying you. You need to let me share your burden. Is it to do with us . . . or our family?"

'C' raised his head and reached out for her hand.

> "You are right . . . again, but it's not just about our family. This one is the grandfather of all problems. All I can say is that the fate of our world now depends entirely on one truly remarkable English girl who became an accidental spy. She is in grave danger of uncovering a nest of problems that could affect the entire world. We had her in the fold . . . and we lost her. Now she is running loose in Australia - running for her life."

"Is it Ruby? You have mentioned her name before, usually after swearing Reggie. My goodness me, how could all that have been allowed to rest on the head of one person? . . . A young woman straight out of training too, I think you said before. Is she one of us . . . or is she yet another damn 'mole'?"

"No, not a 'mole' but you are quite right. Ruby is a new graduate, works within my personal staff. She has survived terrible, terrible events because we took over her life and caused her trauma and misery, three years ago. I brought her in to my team to mentor her in the finer ways of the 'company' and . . . to find out what she knows. We had her covered but someone got to her protector. She has something that many people will do anything to get and if they do get it, through her, they could hold many countries to ransom . . . or destroy them, killing millions of people."

Jenny had nothing more to say. She looked at the children, as they sneakily moved their sprouts to the side of their plates with a look of disgust, with trusty Tigger, their Irish wolfhound standing by quietly, eagerly awaiting his usual secret snack. A phone call broke the tense moment.

"I'll have to grab that. I'm expecting at least some good news out of all this."

Jenny smiled and nodded as she rose up to get the dessert.

"What's new Tian? Where are you?"

"I'm in Perth. I have found our local contact for Jacko's lot, name of Pomphrey and he is saying that she went off on her own. She dumped all the tracking devices we put on her, at the bloody zoo, then the ones from Pomphrey who were also going to follow her. We are trying to get our gear back . . . from a playful orange-haired orang-utan . . . with a damn short temper."

"Bloody hell Tian. What the hell are we on about here? We are treating her like a spoilt wayward child, instead of looking after her and instilling some sort of loyalty to our operations. We are not the bad guys in this world. Anyway, this is too important to mess up. We could all be dead this time next week if that information ever surfaces . . . if it even bloody well exists."

"Well, we're now two agents down - Cathy who was CIA at Heathrow and now our Jack in Perth. We checked all the cameras and boarding passes and still have no leads. We don't know who is after her or what anyone knows about Davis and his mythical papers."

"We must not assume anything Tian. Right then, I will organise a visit to Jacko myself at his premises in Blackpool to see what they know about Ruby's frame of mind on all this. That will be a hard slog too because they are professionals and would probably consider recruiting her themselves," said 'C'.

"Yes, most worked for the 'company' at some stage. I think one avenue of hope, might be to talk with their forgery expert. He would have been responsible for making Ruby's current IDs, based on what Davis may have organised for her. We don't know what name or names she is using for travel."

"Yes . . . I know the one . . . drives that blasted taxis in London, racking up speeding and parking fines, now acting as a 'transporter'. Benfield . . . that's his name. Goes by the codename 'shifter'. Was a bloody good forger too - but an absolute crap field agent."

"Wait on a moment. Right then, I have just been advised, that if Ruby was travelling to the Eastern States, there are only a few ways that she can go. There are cameras everywhere. The Aussies have their cities covered and are monitoring all public transport and have promised to keep in touch with us."

"Don't hold your breath Tian. They think that she murdered two people on their national airline . . . and the CIA will be directing ASIS to hand her over to them. Keep reporting to me directly and I'll give you any resources you need," replied 'C' as he terminated the call.

Tian looked up from her desk at the Perth Airport as one of the surveillance team officers was approaching.

"Good news Tian, we've had some success with the camera recordings and our follow up. The last ten passengers from QF9 have all checked out. Some are on holiday and there are a couple of business people."

"So how does that help us? I mean, if they are all good to go. We have got nothing."

"Just wait a minute. We also looked at the cabin crew and their backgrounds, especially the 'hostie' who was behind them as they were leaving the plane."

"And . . ." urged Tian.

"And, she doesn't exist. She is not part of the regular team. The others had never met her before and they just thought that she was what they call 'deadheading'."

"A very accurate term for what's happened I would say. So what is that exactly?" asked Tian, looking at the photos arranged on the desk.

"Deadheading is when a uniformed flight attendant flies as a passenger, in uniform. Usually they travel like that to work on another flight, or to get back to their home base. They do not work on the flight. We have sent all the information to your people at Heathrow to see if they have a match at their end."

"So what are you saying? . . . That the 'hostie' was the person who killed Jack? Do we know who she is? I can tell you now that our people have confirmed that he was poisoned. It was by a small dart, still lodged into the artery of his neck. Some sort of quick acting nerve agent rendering him paralysed in seconds. So, where did she go after leaving the plane?" pressed Tian looking at the photo of her standing near the exit.

The officer shrugged his shoulders, checked his phone that had indicated a new message and slowly walked away. Tian watched his expression of surprise before he walked back with a faint smile.

"We are dealing with an angel of death. The Heathrow surveillance cameras have just picked up two interesting scenes. It confirms our suspicions about the killing of that CIA girl - who also died in our airline space."

"Cathy Summers, the girl who was stabbed?"

"Yes. It appears that a woman was close behind Cathy and your Ruby . . . both of similar appearance and same coloured coat. The woman was dressed in a particular well-cut outfit and moved away from Cathy as she falls to the ground, many seconds before anyone else reacted. She must have used a serrated plastic knife to do so much damage. Also, this woman then entered the toilets but . . . she did not come out."

"What? But where did she go? How do you mean she didn't come out?" prompted Tian to the officer relishing in his newfound information.

"She went in as a slightly tanned, middle-aged woman with dark hair and that dark grey jacket . . . and she came out as a younger woman, lighter skin tone, with short mousy hair, glasses and wearing . . ."

"A Qantas flight attendant jacket?" finished Tian quietly interrupting his excited delivery.

Tian was beginning to think that they were getting close to finding out who was trying to eliminate Ruby, not for the information, but to stop her finding it, passing it on or using it for her own cause . . . or maybe because they just didn't like her for some totally unrelated reason.

"Your witnesses, the other cabin crew . . . did they detect any accent when she spoke, or was her luggage marked in any way?" asked Tian pensively.

"A few people thought she sounded Eastern European, maybe not as thick as a Russian accent. We lose her after the passenger pickup camera films her getting into a white BMW. We are checking that out now, but it most likely will be a stolen car."

"Hmmm. Thank you for all that . . . err"

"Peter . . . Peter Hastings. I analyse all the data from the camera surveillance locations at the airport, train station and bus port. All our cameras are patched into the police network, so we could get lucky and see this woman at another location around the city."

"Well, thank you Peter. That is a game changer. Let me get you a coffee so we can talk some more. You know there are always rumours about our sides not being totally honest with each other, but times have changed and we must be better at what we do. You can count on me to be fully cooperative and part of your team."

Peter nodded and smiled, but was more excited at the prospect of sharing some time with the famous and strikingly beautiful "Taipan". The ASIS director had told him to keep an eye on her movements, to see if she lets slip any information at all on Ruby and find out why someone would hunt her down on their patch. The exaggerated claims about Tian's past exploits made Peter's skin tingle. Or was it because Tian was so impressionable.

Tian wanted to know how Ruby had exited the Perth area on her own and if she was getting any help with her travels to the Eastern States and the police camera network would come in handy if Peter could identify her in there. Finding Ruby was the only thing on Tian's mind, as the information that she may be withholding must never escape into the dark side of global terrorism.

Another thought crossed her mind. Ruby may think that she had been framed being implicated in the two murders. It was not the first time that Ruby had fallen to such clever work. It was more reason not to trust anyone on her quest to find any documentation left by Davis. Tian now understood why Ruby had not contacted her for help but was still disappointed that their relationship had deteriorated.

Just then, Tian heard the video surveillance team fussing about, talking quietly, secretly, across the room. Tian flicked the switch on her lapel camera to activate the sound amplifier. She heard them mention the name Matylda and what sounded like . . . Morganov.

"Mudarov! Did you get all that . . . and the woman's name Matylda," she whispered into her communicator.

GCHQ had reason to start panicking. Chief analyst, Dale Altridge immediately contacted 'C' with the news and the interim analysis of their backgrounds.

> "Sergei Mudarov . . . he was a member of the Russian Federal Security Service, the FSB, before being outed as a rogue enforcement officer. Apparently, he heavy-handedly secured large oil and gas, and military contracts for his own benefit. From the money laundering, and by financing covert international terrorism, Mudarov seems to have set his sights on much greater rewards, controlling world politics. He also had a murky relationship with some of the 'moles' we discovered three years back and is rumoured to have contacts . . . at Langley and in their military. The person who murdered Cathy Summers and Jack Parton is a close friend of his . . . a woman called Matylda. She's wanted by Interpol and even by the Russians. They are both very bad apples."

> "Christ's sake . . . Keep me informed. We have to act fast," replied 'C' wiping his brow.

Enjoying a long hot shower at the Crown Towers Hotel Casino in the Perth CBD, Matylda Fisher was getting mentally prepared for the evening meeting with her employer, Sergei, who she knew as being a wealthy old Georgian industrialist, with a short fuse and other equally short biometrics. They were to meet in her room. Matylda knew what that meant. Her friends always teased her about becoming an actor 'of sorts'.

She looked at the Qantas flight attendant outfit on the bed, laughing to herself, wondering how no one had picked up the flecks of blood on the jacket and on her shoes. She removed the serrated plastic knife from the inside pocket and washed it, before putting it inside her suitcase ready for another suitable occasion.

Sure enough, at 8pm precisely, a light knock on the door preceded the arrival of Mudarov, who burst it wide open, knocking her across the room. Two burly men quickly closed the door and waited outside. Mudarov stopped and stared at the beautiful woman struggling to regain her feet before him, becoming excited at her wet steaming body and the waft of 'Clive Christian Number One

Imperial Majesty' perfume, which he inhaled slowly. After all, he had paid plenty for it, as well as for the majestic suite in which she was staying.

Matylda pursed her lips as she walked slowly towards him, resulting is his rushed attempt to remove his tight jacket. She gave him a quick kiss before turning away abruptly, at which point Mudarov nearly fell over, removing his belt, letting his trousers fall to the floor.

> "Forgive me Sergei. I have let you down . . . and now I have raised you up again . . . yes? See how we do business, almost a religious experience."

Mudarov was not thinking of business as he fell into her body without saying a word, already out of breath. The guards outside could hear her cries, the screaming and the bumping sounds, as if furniture was being thrown around. They looked at each other, thinking that he was torturing Matylda severely. Moments later, the composed but still naked Matylda opened the door slowly, with the guards expecting that it was their boss wanting to get them to 'clean up' his handiwork. They looked her up and down quickly before turning away to face the opposite wall in the corridor.

> "I think you had better come on in boys and collect what is left of your boss and his . . . enthusiasm. I think he may have slipped a disc or had a heart attack or . . . something equally fatal like that. His last words were, let me see . . . 'Get a doctor, get a doctor, you wild whore, bitch.' Then he stopped breathing, but I think he is coming too . . . well, for me it was just an act . . . of compassion."

Matylda put on a robe, watching on as the two men checked Sergei over and putting on his clothes in a rough manner. He was breathing heavily and was sweating profusely. On seeing Matylda and her aloof expression, he pointed his finger at her, shaking with intense rage.

> "You crazy woman, you could have killed me . . . killed me . . . and yet I would do it all again . . . just to be attacked with such violence and passion," he whispered, catching his breath at last.

"Well, that's the business side of things taken care of Sergei. Now we are even, why don't we go out for dinner and I will tell you what I am going to do with that skinny little Ruby bitch when I catch up with her," said Matylda, stroking the paper opener that was on the desk next to her.

"Wait . . . Wait, we need her alive now, my dear Matylda. You must take her alive. Your orders have changed. We need her to find something . . . something that will make me the king of the entire world. She has it hidden away or she knows how to get it."

Matylda strode over to him slowly, pointing the paper knife at his mid-section, prompting the guards to block her path and Sergei to swallow.

"Why the hell do you want that wiry, starving rabbit alive, Sergei? It is all planned. I will skin her and feed her flesh to my fish and her bones to my lovely Lulu. Why did you want me to kill her in the first place? You are such a tease."

Sergei had fully recovered now and was assuming his usual tough image. He looked at Matylda, put his hand on his heart patriotically and nodded his head slowly.

"That . . . skinny bitch as you say. She and her mentor, Roger Davis, together they worked as a team. Firstly, many years ago, Davis betrayed my sister Kata, by promising her sanctuary in England for her and her son Feliks, as he stole information from her to betray my country. My lovely Kata was tortured and mutilated until she died . . . thrown into the river like a piece of garbage, and when her Feliks sought revenge . . . they were the ones responsible for his murder, in a church confessional of all places.

Then she must also pay for the deaths of many of my comrades in a bomb blast . . . and finally . . . she represents the great pompous MI6. They have wanted to tear me down for many years, ever since I went face to face with their boss. He was in the field back then, in the SAS. That is why I wanted Ruby dead.

But Matylda, for now she must live . . . but only until I get that information that Davis took to his grave. She has it, I know it, I can feel it. It is worth a lot of money to my American friends so they can start another war. Who knows, maybe many wars . . . and yet, maybe I can use it myself. Then you can have her for your tasty snacks . . . after I have had a little talk with her about life."

"More business Sergei? Really, you are becoming a wild animal."

Matylda sensed that her new orders could pay off extremely well, just so long as Sergei did not blow a fuse over the small details.

"Alright Sergei, I will do this . . . only for you, I will do this. Of course, catching this skinny one and then slowly killing her later is going to cost you a lot more."

"Money means nothing to me right now. I can see a bigger prize to be won. You will be rewarded well, as usual. Come, let us go down for dinner and then maybe . . . we can discuss more . . . business plans later."

"Sergei! I need to keep you alive as well. Otherwise I will not get paid. Maybe you should hire a doctor or a vet . . . or buy yourself a hospital. I do have a nice nurse's outfit . . . but it's a bit on the small size and it tends to . . . pop off."

Mudarov's eyes were starting to bulge and glaze over as his breath expired slowly with a wheeze. Matylda took hold of his hand and dragged him out of the room, much to the amusement of his bodyguards.

"You have to feed me Sergei or I cannot do any more business with you . . . and lots of champagne to make me . . . adventurous. Like a big game hunter."

Mudarov's phone alerted him to a new message. He quickly checked it and started getting annoyed, throwing off Matylda's grip on his hand.

"I have to go. Now I have another headache to deal with. It seems that Mr 'C' has sent over his best agent to find out who is killing his people. Maybe they suspect the CIA and not you Matylda. This is good because now you can make it look like Ruby did it. They will not know who to believe. I will organise for dinner on my jet, but first I have to think about what to do with this 'snake lady' who lives up to her name. This is a most unwanted complication."

"Maybe I can I kill her too. Who are you talking about Sergei? Let me strangle her, cook her up in oil and make a handbag from her skin."

"Tian . . . the 'Taipan'. She has slithered into town. No my dear, we must leave here immediately, for otherwise Matylda, you will not last until morning. She is a phantom who strikes from the shadows. Oh, I do hope you like Melbourne my dear. We will be staying at my Crown Casino penthouse tonight. Then . . . you must find this Ruby girl and bring her to me."

At the Perth camera surveillance operations room, five minutes from the hotel, Tian was scouring through the camera recordings with Peter Hastings from all the hotels, city intersections, major public buildings and taxi ranks for the 'Qantas lady' . . . and their own Ruby Peters. Both their biometrics were already in the system to hunt down their targets.

Ten minutes later, the first breakthrough.

"OK, we have your Qantas women at the Crown Towers foyer. Jenkins, get onto them now to find out her room number," said Hastings.

"Right boss."

"Delta Unit, we have confirmation for you now. Crown Towers in East Perth. I'll give you the room number as you go," relayed Hastings to the ASIS team.

"I'll be going too, tell them. I'll meet them at the foyer," interrupted Tian getting up.

There was some more commotion from the display area staff.

"Right, thanks Ben. Well, it looks like your Ruby has been tracked down, at least to a day ago anyway," said Hastings excitedly.

"Where was she? Are you positive it's her?" replied Tian.

They both looked at the video stream on the big monitor.

"Yep, that's her alright. I can tell by her movements. See how she covers her face with that bloody crumpled-up old cap. Where was that taken Peter?"

"It's from the discount shopping centre in West Perth."

There was more cheering in the background.

"Coming through to you now Pete. It's from the taxi rank near that shopping centre, near the little hotel there . . . the Walton or something like that," came the response.

As they watched Ruby walking towards the taxi rank and getting into a taxi, the frame was paused. It was clear and detailed - the taxi plate and cab number clearly visible. Tian memorised the numbers, speaking them out aloud, ready to send as a text message to her own team. She then activated a pre-recorded message bank, to send herself an alarm. Tian looked at it with a surprised look and pretended to be concerned.

"I've got to go Peter. Something has come up at the office and I have to attend. Let me know how you get on. We'll catch up later," said Ruby quickly as she ran down the passageway.

Peter was onto her.

"Ben, get onto Swan Taxis immediately and find out who drove that cab . . . and hold him for questioning. I do not want Tian to get to him first. Oh . . . and also check out that Walton hotel, to see if they know anything."

More information came through from their field unit.

"Peter, I have the woman staying at the penthouse suite, permanently leased by . . ."

"Sergei Mudarov?" interrupted Peter, "Be very careful. He is powerful and his people will protect him with their lives."

Tian raced outside to the nearest Swan Taxi and asked the driver if they knew her friend in Cab 142. She had her answer. The problem now was to find him.

"Is Dinesh working today? I need to speak with him urgently. His life may be in danger. Look . . . here is my British Security pass. It is real. My name is Tian. I am with MI6. He may have become involved with some very dangerous people."

The driver looked very suspicious but had already decided to activate a viable plan that he had prepared for other drivers. He got on the phone to his mate and spoke to him in Hindi, arranging to meet him at a public place.

"Get in and I will take you to him."

The driver kept looking at Tian, feeling for the iron bar that he kept handy in case of being harassed. When they got to the Bentley Shopping Centre, Dinesh was waiting in his cab. Tian approached him as the other driver walked alongside carrying his weapon behind him. Tian had her ID out ready.

"Hello there. My name is Tian and I work for the British Government. I mean no harm to you or your friends. I only want to know what happened to Ruby. She works with me and is in danger. The police and Australian Security are already looking for you . . . to ask you the same thing. Look, here is a photo of you picking her up two days ago."

Dinesh dialled in his cab 'Break Code' to prevent him getting a job. He was about to talk when his radio called him.

"Hello Dinesh. Are you there Dinesh? Please call the base as soon as you finish your break. It is very urgent," boomed the radio.

Immediately, a text message appeared on his scheduler screen.

"See . . . I told you that they want to speak with you."

"I do not know a Ruby. She said her name was Sam and she was very nice. A very nice girl indeed like a super-model. She paid me cash. Why do you want her?" asked Dinesh.

Tian thought for a moment to prevent scaring Dinesh.

"Dinesh . . . Ruby, or Sam as she is now calling herself, is in deep trouble because someone wants to kill her. Did you hear about the Perth Airport troubles a few days ago?"

Dinesh and the other driver started talking very fast and finished by looking at her. They both nodded.

"Well Dinesh, a person was murdered on her plane trip from London to Perth. That attack on the airport, it is linked to the murder. It was supposed to be Ruby. Someone is out to kill her. Can you tell me where you took her? I will not tell anyone else and I advise you to do the same thing. I have no authority in Australia at all with the law. Just tell the police that you took her to the zoo. Do you understand? Now please tell me where she went."

It took a while for Dinesh to talk again, prompted by the other driver. Tian thanked them both for the information and gave each of them one hundred dollars to ease their concerns of her identity.

"Remember not to say anything or else the killer or the police will find her first and may harm you. Tell me, if you were going to the Eastern States from Geraldton, where would you go?"

The other driver started another flurry of Hindi and after nodding to each other, they both agreed on Adelaide, because from there you can go to Melbourne, Sydney or Brisbane by many different ways.

"That's all I want to know. That means other people will come to the same conclusion," said Tian thoughtfully.

Tian walked into the shopping centre to buy some lunch. On the way out, she saw that two black cars had each parked at an angle around the two taxis. The security team had tracked down the cabs by their built-in GPS devices. She watched the security men rush to get back into their cars. Dinesh and his friend had obviously not given her away, which meant that they had not told them about Ruby's trip to Geraldton. If they had, they would have been in trouble with the police, security and their taxi company.

Tian knew that the Geraldton Airport cameras would soon reveal the footage showing that Ruby had caught a flight to Adelaide . . . and the name she had used to pay for the ticket.

At least Peter Hastings, who very much fitted in with ASIO requirements, had no clue that she was using the name Sam

Mowbray . . . and Tian knew that she would also be carrying other credit cards and IDs.

Meanwhile, at the Crown Towers, the ASIS team had drawn a blank after finally accessing the private lift up to the extravagant 'Chairman's Villa' suite. The woman had gone . . . her account paid for automatically by a company called GazTek based in Kyrgyzstan.

A Leer Jet, registered in the name of SergMud was slowly taxiing down the runway. The destination was Melbourne's Tullamarine airport. On the dinner menu was Geraldton crayfish, WAGYU fillet steak, Tasmanian salmon, Beluga caviar and a crate of chilled Moet et Chandon.

> "Did you know that it is fireworks night my dearest Matylda? My dear friend Jacko who worked with MI6 and now competes for work against my company – I find that they are the same criminals who helped Ruby to escape. We could have taken her on the day she arrived . . . but their Mr Pomphrey thought otherwise. We have infiltrated their group and know this . . . and where they are hiding," said Sergei softly rubbing his chin.

At the Malaga bunker where Jacko's Perth team were holding out, their security cameras showed two cars pulling up right outside their perimeter fencing. The occupants of one car drove close up to the gated entrance and parked the car with the engine still running, before jumping into the other car and speeding off. The bunker was soundproofed and the other crew did not hear the squealing tyres.

Automatic alarms had activated just moments before a massive explosion tore through their compound. The noise was deafening, and a huge crater replaced where the car had been.

Pomphrey was no more. He had been tinkering with the old motorbike that Davis had once used, preparing to take it home with him to England. He was two months away from being 'deposited' in a Whitehall office.

Everything seemed eerily quiet as the resulting fire raged around the area, threatening other buildings in the vicinity. Then slowly, the distant wailing of police, ambulance and fire engines started to become a cacophony of rising and falling sirens . . . with smoke and flames roaring into the warm night sky.

In Blackpool England, Jacko was out getting fish and chips for his crew of Bill and Jamie, from Joe Salmon's chippy on Coronation Street. It was his shout and everyone had prepared for the usual dose of 'extras'. His two assistants were preparing to again suffer in silence as they ate his version of an iconic dish . . . with his predictable double salt and vinegar, covered with big splodges of tomato sauce.

As he approached the office, he stopped at the corner, concerned that three motorbikes had pulled up outside the office in a line. They riders were all dressed in black, with balaclavas around their faces under tinted visors.

Suddenly, each drew out their UZI 9mm submachine guns and started firing, sweeping the scene in a criss-cross pattern, shattering the glass, walls and everything inside. The people in the street scattered, taking shelter behind walls and cars. Jacko reached for his pistol, hidden in a pouch attached to a leather shoulder harness.

The sounds of police sirens approaching, unnerved Jacko as he steadied his hand, firing five rounds into the men. One of them fell instantly. Another, wounded in the shoulder, managed to ride off, weaving erratically down the road. The third man turned around to shoot back, leading Jacko to think that he may have been recognised.

Jacko ducked down as the man revved the engine, riding his bike straight towards him, shooting erratically after hitting the curb and stalling the bike. The next thing he heard was the firing of multiple rounds of single shots, as the man stumbled past him, crashing into the now shattered shop window, which injected shards of glass into his failing body. The police had arrived.

There was just enough time for Jacko to quickly survey the scene and move further up the road. He realised that both his lads inside were dead, judging by the damage. Young Bill had only just been engaged too.

At least he had killed one of the assailants and wounded another, with the police and the glass window taking care of the third man. The Swiss Bus Company head office was no more. Police barricades were already up and more personnel were arriving to sort through the mess and to interview any witnesses.

It was time to make a call to 'C' to get the necessary resources to find the remaining gunman, now wounded and probably bleeding profusely before he vanished into the void . . . or retrieve his body for further identification.

This man would surely know something about who authorised this professional attack and how they knew the location of their headquarters . . . given sufficient persuasion.

Jacko would see to it that extracting information from him was going to be a long process . . . payback time, for killing his friends.

All Roads Lead

A group of pre-school children were out on their regular morning walk, holding hands and keeping close to their much loved teacher, when they caught sight of a white campervan passing through their country town. They started pointing, waving and laughing at the sole occupant who was singing loudly to 'Somewhere over the Rainbow' at the top of her voice, but with different words and fill-in sounds. Ruby waved back excitedly with a happy smile until they faded into the distance.

The cool air conditioning was working a treat in the thirty-five degree summer heat – almost too cold now. She stared at the indoor temperature reading again to confirm it was only fourteen degrees. Rather than mess with the dials and switches, she turned it off.

The last signpost indicated that she had passed through Tailem Bend, just 'down the road' from Murray Bridge, according to a local man she had met on the way. It was actually twenty-five kilometres.

The going was already getting tough for Ruby, having travelled nearly one hundred kilometres over a good three hours, from Adelaide. Service stations were proving a popular stop-off point to collect more cheese snacks and a few cans of various fizzy drinks. The tourist brochure from Adelaide showed that it would only take two hours to Tailem Bend but then she had been lost once or twice. The people all seemed very friendly, waving, tooting their horns and flashing their lights at her as she made her way forward.

> "Only another two thousand kilometres to go," she muttered, looking at the fading light and the isolated road ahead.

Ruby pulled over to a layby with a picnic table under a tall tree to check her large crumpled up map. She thought that it would be nicer to sit outside rather than at her small table in the van. However, opening the door was like walking into an oven and it was not long before those annoying bushflies had invaded her space, their sole mission being to inspect every traveller's nose, mouth and eyes.

She ran over to the table to sit down, covering her snack and drink with her head whilst wafting away the flies, trying not to breathe through her mouth. It was so hot. The drink can was awash with beads of icy water, condensed from the humidity in the air.

The food soon became the new mustering point for thousands of local ants as she batted away not only the flies now but also some very persistent wasps. They were each trying to grab any moisture or nutrients they could find, regardless of who was protecting it. It was then, that she looked back at the van.

Hanging from the roof was a huge advertising sock, the type that grows with a rush of air and then folds down again. It had a funny yellow face with red hair and a toothy smile. She remembered it blowing around at the last service station . . . and reversing into a tight spot to go to the shop area.

She raced back to the van, throwing her picnic fare into a waste bin and closing the door quickly to stop any more flies from getting in. Then she waited a few seconds before getting out to pull the toothy canvas monster off the van from where it had snagged, bundling it into a roll, and leaving it next to the wood pile, set up for BBQs.

Once back inside the van, she screwed up the map so that it only showed the area where she was travelling. It soon occurred to her that a lot of time would be wasted travelling in the van. It had sounded so easy when explained to her by the locals, who all agreed that three ten-hour days was more than enough to get to Brizzy. Her priority was still to inspect her portfolio there and sell what she could . . . after a thorough search for any hidden secrets – if there were any. She also had to avoid running into her assassin.

After Brisbane, the next plan was to travel to the Royale marina near Hobart. That would require a further three thousand kilometres to cover plus a ferry trip across the wild Bass Strait – with an overnighter being preferred. She finally realised that her original plans, based on wild assumptions of time and distance were over.

The more she thought about Davis and his antics, the more she thought that if anywhere was going to produce results, it would be on a yacht that can move day or night, without official scrutiny. It would also double as a private oasis from the mainstream of modern city life. It had Davis written all over it.

A new plan emerged spontaneously. It sounded to her, even crazier than the last. She decided to head back to Murray Bridge for the night then hire a local plane to fly her to Melbourne, from where she could travel to Hobart. Whoever was following her trail would not expect her to fly again or even be in Melbourne.

Wafting away more flies that had hitched a ride, she made the trip back in thirty minutes, looking for a suitable motel with all the basic amenities. Camping was fun for some people when on holidays - but Ruby was not on holidays, and she was not having much fun.

The woman at reception watched as Ruby parked the van. She had trouble understanding why it was not at the caravan park next door. The van eventually came to a halt, parked almost straight, but still protruding into three car bays. Ruby slammed the door and looked relieved at her effort until she glanced at the white parking-bay lines. She wondered if the rental company would send someone from Adelaide to pick up the van or if they had someone local to take care of it. It was a busy tourist route after all.

"Hi there, do you have a room for the night. I'm done for the day and just want a good sleep and definitely a nice meal," sighed Ruby.

The woman looked at Ruby then back to the van.

"They're a bugger to drive those vans. Had one myself and travelled a fair bit in it with my dog. Had to put it down."

They both stared at each other.

"Nah – the dog. The dog was what got put down. It got himself a tick in his neck and was real bad, poor bugger," she continued.

"Oh, I'm very sorry about that. I am Kay by the way and I have just travelled up from Adelaide heading to Brisbane . . . but now I have to get to Melbourne by tomorrow night. I have to report there for a job that's just come up," said Ruby slowing down as she went, to match the pace of the conversation.

The woman looked at her again and then back to the van, unsure of what to say next. She was about to say something, but then held back, deep in her thoughts.

"So, do you have a room for me?" continued Ruby.

"Yes, I can fix you up with a room. Just you is it love?"

"Just me and for the one night."

The woman bent down to pick up the key for room 25 which was at the end of a row, then pushed some paperwork towards Ruby.

"Sixty dollars for the night. I can give you some sandwiches or a hot pie if you are hungry. There's coffee, milk and some beer and wine in the minibar. Now tell me Kay . . . how are you proposing to get to Melbourne so quick? Your van doesn't go that fast. Even old Ted can't drive that fast."

"I thought I could leave it here and . . ."

"Nah, you can't do that. Old Ted will go off his head."

"No, I mean with the hire company . . . are they here at all?" continued Ruby.

"Well, there is old Jack down at the servo who could take it back for you I suppose . . . but then how's he going to get back home again?"

"Don't you have an agent for Britz campers in Murray Bridge or somewhere close by? No wait, I'll phone them up tomorrow to see what they can do."

"Yeah, you can phone them alright . . . but I don't think they will want to come all the way up from Adelaide to pick it up. Anyway, how are you going to get to Melbourne then? No van . . . and the train will take about eleven hours."

"Don't you have an airport?" asked Ruby briskly.

The woman laughed, shaking her head.

"You're in Murray Bridge love, not the big smoke. Now, I tell you what I think. Take the train. It leaves from here tomorrow at 1020am and arrives in Melbourne around 7pm.

It's called the 'Southern Cross' and it will cost you about two hundred dollars, this time of year."

"The 'Southern Cross', blimey, I could have taken that from Perth in the first place. Right then, I'll pay you for the room and catch the train tomorrow," proposed Ruby confidently.

The woman looked at the van and the back to Ruby who was predicting her next question.

"The van will be picked up by Britz once I contact them. I will leave it at the caravan park instead. You never know, there may be someone wanting to take it back to Adelaide in the park," continued Ruby.

The woman started shaking her head again.

"Nah, I can't see that happening. No one from here wants to go to Adelaide, not even old Ted . . . maybe Melbourne, for a few days to take a bit of a break from the missus . . . Nah, just get that company to pick it up . . . but it will cost you."

Ruby took her key after fixing up the paperwork and started to leave the office, with the woman still staring at the van. She opened the door and walked towards it. One of the cleaners was looking through the back window.

"You can have it if you like. It's all paid up for three days, providing it goes back to Adelaide. I am leaving it here so I can get the train to Melbourne. It's supposed to be dropped off in Brisbane, but I reckon the firm will send someone from Adelaide to collect it."

The woman was from some Asian country as far as Ruby could determine, possibly from the Philippines or maybe Indonesia.

"G'day, I was just checking it out. That would be a great van to travel in if I had the money. Better than stuck here with old grumpy bum in there," she replied.

Ruby was quick to think of another twist to her plan.

"Look, I'll pay you extra to take it to Adelaide if you can take time off. How about five hundred dollars cash? Would that do it? I mean, you have to get back here again, I suppose," offered Ruby quietly.

The woman's eyes lit up. She looked at the van, then back towards the office with her mouth open, thinking about the possibilities.

"You're on. I can drive there with my boyfriend and take a sickie. Oh, my name is Layla. I was born in Sydney but did some study at the Uni in Adelaide some years ago, which I am completing online. My family came here from the Philippines many years ago."

"Hi, and I'm Kay . . . from England as you probably guessed. What are you studying?"

"Yeah, I thought you were a Pom . . . no offence Kay," replied Layla, "I'm doing a degree in sociology."

"Wow that's cool. Well this will be a story you can write about in the future. You know, naïve English girl gets lost in Australian outback. OK then, let's get this all sorted then. I have to catch the train tomorrow. Not my best idea because I don't like trains, but then . . . that's all there is," replied Ruby testing for other options.

"You can catch the bus at 8am you know. That is what I would do and you will be in Melbourne at the same time as the train anyway . . . about 7pm. Yep, I would definitely catch the bus. It takes a bit longer, but it sets off earlier. Then you can sit back and relax, not having to worry about that van of yours," said Layla still staring at the marvel of Ruby's crazy parking.

"I was just getting used to backing it in," joked Ruby, "Are you going to tell the motel owner that you are going away for a few days?"

"Nah, she can get her arse into gear and do some cleaning herself for a change. She doesn't do much else other than sit at that counter, watching the world go by. I'll take a sickie."

They both had a quiet laugh before going to Ruby's room to organise the transport of the van back to Britz. Layla's boyfriend, Robert worked at the caravan park next door and jumped at the chance of travelling, rather than looking after other travellers. He was also studying – for an agricultural science degree and wanted to own a farm one day. He told them to drive the van around to the caravan park for the night, so that they could have an early start. He seemed all right and was even more enthusiastic when given the money for their trip.

"Don't let me down, please. I am going to return this way after my time in the Easter States and will call in on you if you have not returned it. I am trusting you both with quite a bit of money, especially being total strangers. I do not want to have to worry about this on my travels. You have two days to drive it on a two-hour trip. Make the most of it. Happy camping!"

Ruby could now cover her trail again, knowing that whoever was after her would now know that she had hired a campervan, heading for Brisbane. Layla drove Robert's car to give Ruby a lift back to the motel, stopping off for a Hungry Jack's burger combo. Ben Sandford was right about the taste.

Settling in for the night, Ruby turned on the television to the channel 24 ABC News station. The tone and pictures of the news story caused her to listen closely. The reporter was explaining the cause of an explosion in the Perth suburb of Malaga.

"In what has been described as an act of terrorism today, the premises of 'Swizbus', an offshoot of the British transport company 'Swiss Bus Company' based in Lancashire, has been destroyed by a massive car bomb explosion. There were no survivors from the building, which was totally demolished. There are also reports that three people have been injured from neighbouring properties, some with extensive burns."

Ruby was in shock, thinking quickly about how it may concern her own safety. Then she thought about Pomphrey, Ben Sandford and the other people who worked with them . . . all now dead. It was becoming a regular occurrence for her to be leaving a trail of death and destruction . . . but there was more to come. The newsreader was crossing over to their reporter in London.

"The head of British intelligence operations has also confirmed that the head office of the 'Swiss Bus Company' in Blackpool has been attacked by a group of three masked gunmen armed with what has been described by witnesses as submachine guns, in an apparent escalation of violence against this company. It appears at this stage, that the owner and two of his staff are dead. The motive is unknown at this stage. Locals described the owner, Jack O'Reilly, as a warm and compassionate person who had operated his transport company for many years, often donating his coaches for school and charity outings. In the Middle East . . ."

Ruby turned off the television and grabbed a can of 'whisky and coke' from the fridge, drinking it down quickly. In her mind, the covering of her tracks was a priority. These people had obviously used extensive and professional resources. Now that she had ditched the van and told the motel owner she was catching the train, that only left Layla and Robert to believe she was not going to Melbourne, but was now headed to Sydney. She phoned Layla who was sitting inside the van with Robert and a bottle of whisky.

"Hi Kay, I hope you haven't had second thoughts. We are going to sleep in the van tonight, ready to go early."

"No Layla, everything is fine. I just thought I would tell you that the fridge has to be left open when you take the van back, that is all. Oh, and I will be travelling to Sydney on the train after all. It seems that my job interview is at the company's head office in . . . Pitt Street?"

"Yeah, that's right in the centre of the city. Good luck with the interview and thank you again for letting us use the van . . . and for trusting us."

"Thanks Layla. Have a great trip. Goodbye," finished Ruby.

Ruby reached into the fridge for another cold drink. This time it was a 'vodka and orange'. She drank it all and flopped onto the bed, pulling the top sheet around her. She spent the night drifting in and out of sleep making sure she did not miss the bus. She was looking forward to travelling in her luxury seat to Melbourne, knowing that she could doze off or just relax with a drink, without anyone caring.

Her thoughts turned to Jacko and his men. Ruby could fully understand Roger Davis keeping to himself. There is no such thing as retirement once entrenched into the murky world of intelligence security.

At the back of her mind was the urge to contact Tian and get things sorted between her and the 'company'. The reality was that it was too dangerous to communicate anything to anyone. She also had a special understanding with her Dad, Harry, that if he received a certain coded message, it would mean that she had gone to ground or had faked her own death in order to escape. It had not come to that yet.

Tian had arrived in Adelaide on a late flight from Perth after acting on information from Dinesh who had driven Ruby to Geraldton. He had advised Ruby to fly to Adelaide to escape the long divide between east and west. Tian had analysed Ruby's position and way of thinking. Risking a connecting flight from Adelaide to Brisbane was too dangerous, as she would have to sit at the airport amongst all the security cameras and undercover intelligence officers, who always check waiting passengers within the boarding gate areas.

Going directly to a bus depot or train station would be equally easy to track her. The only options left were hitchhiking with strangers or truckies, hiring a car, or using a campervan with built-in accommodation.

Tian tried several places in order of likelihood, offering her fake ID as that of Detective Inspector Julia Field from the Australian Federal Police.

> "Bingo", whispered Tian to herself, after she placed Ruby's photo on the counter at Britz in Adelaide and they confirmed that she had hired a van.

> "Can you give me the registration number and description of the van please and I'll be on my way?"

Tian needed to find Ruby fast and she also had to cover her tracks in case she was being followed. It was late night shopping and the motorcycle shop around the corner was about to close. A 650cc Yamaha had just come back from a sales run and both salesman and buyer were eager to finalise their sale.

Tian calmly walked up to the counter and removed the keys. A quick look towards the office and she had the bike coasting away out of view. The helmet was hanging off the handlebar, so with a quick start, away she left on low revs before accelerating into the busy traffic.

Tian was moving like the Roman Legions who marched all day and all night at a quick pace, coming upon their enemy with complete surprise. At least she was on the same side as Ruby and now only one-step behind, but she could not work out a strategy to convince Ruby to come back into the fold. The moment of contact was now getting closer.

Meanwhile in the CIA operations room at Pine Gap, Joe Goldberg and David Reichmann were arguing with their counterparts over at Langley headquarters. Director Steve Miller, had taken over operation 'Dormant' and was on a conference call to the two apparently inept data analysts, flanked by the heads of army, navy and air force.

"No Joe, don't tell me that you lost her again. Don't you dare say that your trillion-dollar pile of shit is not working or has somehow gotten a mind of its own. Tell anything . . . but not that crap!"

"We had her in Adelaide Sir . . . sure as hell, the 'sat' pictures had her coming out of the airport and getting into a cab. We called in the field support guy, a Jake Coltrane, immediately and he followed our call on where the cab was headed. Unfortunately, she must have got out along the way because she . . ."

"You lost her . . . riding in a damn cab? Did you get the cab company name and find out where she got out, or was that put in the too hard basket as well?"

"Eventually we did, yeah. City Cabs and she got out in a business district, near to the bus depot and quite a few car yards and hire companies. Jake went around quite a few places, which were near to closing time. The photo he had of her was from London . . . and who knows what name she was travelling under."

"Certainly not you guys. Apparently, you know Jack shit. Well, the news from the Aussies is that she was travelling on the plane as Sandra Jacobs. They also came up with the name Sam Mowbray from some apartment she stayed in when in Perth. Hell . . . this girl's got more names than a   pizza menu."

"Yeah Steve, I think the Brits trained her real good. Good looking broad too."

The defence chiefs were looking very frustrated at all this casual banter, staring at Miller who appeared to be making light of the situation. Miller pressed on.

"We have her renting a Britz campervan going to Brisbane, this time calling herself Alice Palmer. Apparently, she spent the night at Murray Bridge as Kay. The locals say she caught the train from there to Melbourne this morning. So get your 'sat' locked onto that train all the way to Melbourne and be ready to pick her up at 7pm from the Flinders Street Station. Our people will be there to follow her movements. She is obviously making her way to get those papers left by that Davis guy. Do not lose her this time . . . this may be our last chance to get a lock onto her before she finds the information we are looking for. We will throw everything at this if need be."

"Geez, she must be some big deal then, this girl from England. What the hell did she do wrong?"

"Look at it like this Joe . . . she is going to be the catalyst or the disabler for an all-out nuclear war . . . so, yeah Joe . . . she is a big deal . . . to too many people . . . and we have to get to her first. Don't lose her!"

The Army Chief had left the room and was already on his phone to relay the information to his outsider partner.

Sergei Mudarov commenced making plans to send Matylda on a new errand. He could not believe that Ruby would be in the same city at the same time.

Facing Up

There was much excitement from waiting families and friends around the Melbourne bus station as the interstate bus from South Australia arrived just after 7pm. The passengers however, were getting off slowly and awkwardly after sitting down for lengthy periods, covered in crumbs and spilt drinks.

It was still twenty-four degrees and the driver's thoughts were on sinking his first ice-cold beer for the night. He too slowly emerged from the bus, aching and feeling the heat after being in the air-conditioning for too long.

As all the security services thought that Ruby was catching the train, there was no surprise greeting party waiting for the bus. The passengers were now mingling in with the rest of the bus station melee after collecting their bags . . . but there was one woman who stood out from the crowd, standing alone, hands on hips, shaking her head.

"She is not here. Did you check the train station? I doubt that she would have caught the train. I would have bet my life on it . . . but then, here we go again . . . No bloody Ruby," whispered Tian into her communicator.

"Nothing at the train station either Tian. She has pulled off another 'swifty' . . . quite out of the guidelines for 'company' fieldwork. Your star pupil has fooled everyone again, looking at all the feds and intelligence bods searching around the train station," replied the MI6 coordinator.

Tian saw the bus driver limping along to the depot office, straining and stretching his back and neck to get some relief.

"Excuse me. I saw you come in on the bus from South Australia just now. My name is D.I. Julia Field. I am with the Federal police. Have you seen this woman? Did she get on your bus from Murray Bridge this morning?"

The driver looked at Tian closely. He was surprised that the young woman was in any sort of trouble. He just wanted to have a drink with his mates.

"Yes she did? Why? She is such a nice girl. Anyway, I dropped her off at the hospital not far from here to see her grandmother. She looked very sad . . . was worried about her gran's operation."

"Yes . . . I bet she was. Well, thank you for your help. Oh, it is nothing serious by the way. We just need to give her some information about her family back in England. Thanks."

Tian reported her findings and went to look for a café to think things over, as Ruby was now becoming an embarrassment to her own skills. She found a coffee shop not far away and sat there quietly, mulling over the characteristics of both Ruby and Roger Davis. She had a feeling that Ruby would catch the bus but not that she would get off early. It was now 8pm and her call from 'C' came through.

"Tian, we have some more news. She caught the bus and got off at a taxi rank north of the station, near a hospital."

"Right Sir, I have just confirmed the same thing. Any clues as to where she is going? I do not think she is going to Brisbane. Maybe Sydney, now that is a possibility. She can't show her face at any city location or modes of transport because they are all covered by the Feds and intelligence people."

"She has a plan for sure and is keen to throw us off the trail. The CIA bombed out at the train station by the way. We are monitoring their communications. They contacted me a short time ago to tell me about Mudarov. The word is out Tian. We have to find Ruby quickly. What would Davis be doing in Australia? Did he ever give any indication as to what he did on his little jaunts?"

Tian sighed, thinking of all the times she had close contact with Davis whilst on surveillance duties.

"He mentioned the warm weather, spending time on the beach, something about beautiful scenery and a big or grand mountain, food, wine, sailing . . ."

"Sailing Tian? That means being on the coast."

"Well, all the capital cities are on the coast over here Sir. I wonder where he went sailing. You know, owning your own boat would be the ideal way to lose yourself in a city. No roads or checkpoints and nobody to bother you. Hmmm, now there's a plan for the future," laughed Tian.

"Probably why I could never get in touch with the blighter when he was on holidays. He just dropped off the radar for a few weeks. Yes Tian. That is worth following up. I'll get GCHQ to have a go at looking through all the transport boarding areas around Melbourne for any hint of her, no doubt using those fake IDs given to her by Jacko's mob."

"How is he by the way? Jacko . . . he would have to be feeling very lucky. He must have just escaped by seconds from that attack in Blackpool . . . and his base in Perth that was destroyed. Do we know who did it?"

"No, but he contacted me, yesterday in fact. Very upset at the loss of his people . . . most of them ex-military and 'company' of course. He seems to think that the destruction of his operation is linked to the deaths of Cathy and Jack. Smells like he had a 'mole' in the works. We will have to see who is missing when they have identified all the bodies. I think we will take him back into the fold. I may even send him out to help you. He is a top operator Tian and probably knew Davis as much as anyone else. He could be very useful to you."

"Yes, I think he should get out here now. I will get back to you when I catch up with Ruby. It's only a matter of time."

"And time is running out . . . I'll get more information about Davis and his holidays. GCHQ is filtering the available passenger data from all Melbourne departure points. Use whatever resources you need Tian. Watch out for our trigger-happy American friends . . . and find out who killed Cathy and Jack. That assassin needs to be taken down, her outfit identified and the ringleader exposed. We have her name as Matylda, but of course it won't be her real name."

Tian thought more about the scenery, mountain and sailing clues left by Davis through casual references to colleagues. Looking around, she noticed one of the tourist kiosk staff, quite a nice-looking young man, eating a meal across the walkway, now looking a little wary as Tian approached him rather forcefully.

"Hi there, do you mind if I ask you a question about tourist locations, only I noticed that you are part of the information centre?"

"Yes, sure. No problem. For a moment there, I thought you were going to . . . no, well . . . I'm writing a crime novel in my spare time and I get a bit edgy . . . being in the zone and all that rubbish. So, what do you want to know then?"

"I'm sorry if I frightened you so, with my directness. Sometimes I appear . . . too eager. My job is to extract information from people so that my company can stay ahead of the field. I have learnt to cut to the chase."

The young man was thinking quickly about how this was heading. It was almost like living out part of his story.

"Not by chopping off fingers or anything like that I hope," he said half-smiling.

"No, not today anyway . . . and that would be the Yakuza, Japanese men and they are heavily tattooed. I am a woman, I assure you," she answered straight-faced, raising her eyebrows suggestively.

"Yes I can see that . . . I mean being a woman and all that," he blurted out nervously.

Tian bent down to his eye level, delivering a close-up of her breasts, wafting the most hallucinating, warm, orange-perfume towards him that he had ever imagined.

"See any tattoos down there?" breathed Tian with pursed lips.

The young man was now feeling warm and bothered by her fresh approach, feeling awkward but enthralled at having such a beautiful woman make an obvious play for his attention.

Tian moved around to the empty seat next to him, pulling it closer, pinching a chip from his plate.

"Right then, so where would I go in Australia where there is superb scenery, a big or backdrop of a mountain and somewhere I could go sailing . . . in a quiet area with no customs or port interference?" she breathed quietly with wide eyes.

"Well . . . well one place comes to mind immediately. So, why do you not want to have any official interference with your boat then? What do you want to do there? You know . . . I think . . ."

Tian cut him off with a demanding look that probably still haunts him to this day.

"One word, one word answer. Where?"

"Hobart."

Tian smiled at him and placed her hand on his thigh.

"Thank you for helping me. If I have any more questions . . . I know where to find you, don't I . . ."

"T . . . Toby."

"Maybe we can have dinner . . . or something . . . next time," breathed Tian, licking her lips and moving her hand up and down his leg.

Tian stood up quickly but walked away slowly. She had one more look at the open-mouthed Toby before crossing the road, smiling to herself, knowing that Toby had warmed to her advances. She breathed in and out slowly.

"I am so sorry dear Ilya, but it is now time for me to move on," she whispered to herself.

Tian sent an encrypted message to 'C' explaining the new developments, then organised transport to Hobart by Virgin Airlines, as they both concluded that Qantas would not want any more dramas happening, especially on home soil . . . and with local security watching out for her and Ruby.

The Federal police, ASIO and a team of CIA operatives had waited until the last passenger got off the train at the Flinders Street train station before checking the interior. Langley was viewing the scene via live satellite coverage, with Miller up close to the screen waiting for the arrest to take place. He had already obtained an 'understanding' that Ruby was to be moved directly to the airport for transfer to the U.S.

"Where is she? Where the hell is she . . . anyone? Did you see her get off? Who can tell me something? Anything?" shouted Miller in a rage.

After a few seconds, there was a reply back from Agent Mullins at the scene. Having showed the staff Ruby's photo, he had confirmed the worst.

"Mullins here Sir . . . I can confirm that she was never on the train. Repeat . . . she never got on the train."

"So where the hell is she then? We must have had her under surveillance from Murray Bridge . . . yes . . . no . . . I mean, what are we running here . . . a freaking freaks show?"

There was no answer. The Australians put out another APB to all transport venues, but they did not know where she was.

Flinders Street station was now quiet again. The team of CIA field agents had scoured all around the nearby Melbourne business district, checking bars, cafes and clubs. They now knew for sure that she did not catch the train because the satellite imagery could not find her getting on or off the train at any point on its travels.

The chiefs at Langley were beginning to question the competence of their field operatives with such a simple task. Miller began to think like Ruby, weighing up all the options.

"She caught the bus guys. She caught the damn bus. Why were we not watching the bus? Get hold of that driver and find out what he knows . . . now!"

Miller began weighing up his options. It included getting in touch with MI6. Some sort of compromise to their previous unsupportive dealings had to be resolved. This was too serious to be playing games. ASIO were busy analysing all the security cameras around Melbourne for a facial recognition match. It was an obvious time for all parties to come to the table, to set down the known facts about Davis and his presumed secret papers and find them before Mudarov.

At another café in the heart of Melbourne, a distraught figure was brooding over the day's turn of events. Matylda had yet to inform Sergei that Ruby did not get off the train as expected. She had searched everywhere and had stayed behind for a couple of hours in case Ruby was hiding out for time.

She imagined a stinging rebuke from Sergei, for another failure or a sound beating before he had his way with her. He only allowed so much from his expendable close cohorts . . . with lying and disrespect high up on the list of 'terminal' offences. She knew that he would be thinking that she was making up her story. Once he had made up his mind, he would never admit he was wrong.

Matylda decided to wait it out overnight, to work out whether she had overstayed her welcome, maybe the time to relinquish her investments and go into hiding. Deep down she accepted that like any secret organisation, mafia or terrorist group . . . there is no place to retire from the dark world of greed and power . . . or Mudarov.

In the meantime, after getting off the bus, Ruby had raced quickly to a taxi rank and jumped in the first cab, asking the driver to take her to the TT Line ferry terminal in St Kilda, where the 'Spirit of Tasmania' was shortly leaving for Devonport in Tasmania. She had booked a deck seat during the bus trip, after considering that it was highly unlikely Davis would leave any personal papers at his house or car in Brisbane.

Ruby was now working her fourth and last false identity, under the name of Angelica Rossetti, a PHD student in linguistics travelling to Hobart for a conference at the University of Tasmania.

Once on-board the ferry, Ruby made her way to the cinema, armed with a most delicious selection of sandwiches and chocolate milk for the trip to 'Tassie'.

Placing her beret over her forehead, she peered out at the running of 'Dunkirk', swivelling her eyes around to view her surroundings, sandwich in mouth.

She could feel the adrenalin kick in at times during the movie and imagined her own rescue with similar consequences after being extricated from the life she was currently living. At least she was safe for the moment and was having second thoughts about her negative view of the 'company' and her abandonment of duty . . . and Tian.

Red Phones

It was midnight in Vauxhall Cross, London and early evening in Langley, Virginia. A conference call was underway by the anxious security chiefs of the two nations. It was time to call a truce on their differences and come clean with the looming threat they were facing.

They were mulling over a report from Peter Hastings, ASIO Australia, about the suspect match between the murders of Cathy Summers and Jack Parton. The evidence pointed to an unknown woman, now linked to the infamous Sergei Mudarov. ASIO were investigating her movements around Australia but her present whereabouts were unknown.

Mudarov had travelled to the Crown Casino complex via his private jet and there was a scramble to obtain any video of the woman being there, after arriving in Melbourne aboard the jet, or entering the Crown Casino. She was most likely in disguise. Surveillance had been set up to prevent anyone leaving the penthouse, without authority from ASIO.

"Look here 'C', putting all of our cards on the table . . . we know that your agent Peters . . . Ruby . . . is the only thing that is stopping this Mudarov from obtaining, what . . . some sort of list of explosive devices? What are they and do you know for sure that they even exist?" asked Steve Miller surrounded by his military chiefs and security analysts at Langley.

'C' looked cautiously at his second in command, Simon Bentham, before answering. They had come up with some very disquieting information about the number of people in attendance on the American side.

"I am not prepared to discuss any further information that we have obtained, until you remove only the highest security clearance personnel from your present staff. I think that we have an informer amongst us who is passing information on to Mudarov. May I suggest at this stage, that we only include the senior directors and senior 'intel' analyst at this time? No military personnel at this stage. We are not at war . . . yet."

There was silence at the other end.

"One moment 'C'. I will do as you say at this point, but what you tell me must be substantial enough to exclude any of my hand-picked team members. I respect your judgement and . . . well, give me five minutes."

"Thank you Director Miller. As I say, this is extremely sensitive information that must not reach the outside world," responded 'C'.

There was much arguing and resentment in the American camp, especially between the military chiefs. The only people remaining were Miller, his deputy and the lead-security data analyst. After the door had closed behind them, Miller breathed in and slowly exhaled before listening to just how much the British knew about Mudarov and the explosives.

"Ok 'C', we are secure at this end. You will now only be talking with me, Max Carter my deputy, and data analyst director, Janet Paisley."

"Right then, let us proceed quickly, by my talking you through what we have, what we think we have, and finally . . . what we are currently doing about it. I must say at this stage that our only lead is through one of our own agents, Ruby Peters, who has been through hell both before and during her time with us at MI6. I am sure you have a full dossier on her yourselves and . . . well there is some misunderstanding about her role in your international affairs that need clearing up.

I am talking about that incident concerning Ruby and two of your rogue agents and some stolen diamonds . . . and further incidents, which caused the deaths of those same two agents and now the tragic death of Cathy Summers at Heathrow. Well, let me just say that she has some interesting history with your organisation that has been misconstrued and exaggerated," explained 'C' briskly with raised eyebrows, looking at Simon's expression.

"She must be some sort of 'Susan Storm' with so much conviction and energy for fighting and survival there 'C'. Yes, we certainly have a library of information on your Ruby and her antics. I must admit too, that we are extremely angry and have been seeking recompense for her actions and yet . . . we are somehow in awe of her fortitude, in carrying out such masterful strokes of strategy. Yes, we have noted her unfortunate losses along the way . . . her boyfriend Eric for starters, Davis her mentor and so many more people around her. However . . . this must be put to one side while we listen to what you have to say about her role in our present emergency."

"Just on that, before we proceed, I can assure you that your anger is not justified, in what is really a snowball effect of her being in the wrong place at the wrong time three years ago. Now then, that aside and moving on . . . you mentioned Davis. At one time he was our best agent . . . thorough, meticulous for details . . . and one for seeing the darker side of power plays destroyed," said 'C' sadly.

"Roger Edward Davis. We have many tales and evidence of his work here too 'C'. Some talk very highly of him. Strange that he made friends with so many foreign agents . . . even those who wanted to kill him, but I believe he turned many a fine foreign agent over to your side too, including Major Ilya Kasparov and Jin Shi Tian, that incredible Chinese woman . . . but please go on."

'C' laughed softly, remembering Davis as a stickler for detail and the huge amount of paperwork he produced from his endeavours.

"Davis recruited Ruby as a sixteen year old from school, along with her Eric . . . way too early and tragically so troublesome for all around her. Anyway, he became her mentor and protected her for the remainder of his life. He sometimes waited outside her house for days whilst the 'Cigar Club' was actively trying to kill her for those damn diamonds. Getting to the point . . . we think that he entrusted his 'final paperwork' and his accumulated assets to Ruby and Eric. With Eric's demise, that leaves Ruby alone to carry out what

Davis has surely documented in his 'secret place', if you believe like me that he would have done so."

"We all have a secret place in our line of work 'C'. It is the only part of us that remains untouched . . . until we meet our maker," replied Miller.

"We think that Davis had his secret place or fox-hole in Australia to which Ruby is now headed. At this point in time, we are sure she has no idea what will be there . . . and that is also a worry. Davis confided in me once that the world is not a safe place. Well, we all know that I told him, otherwise you would be out of a job . . . but he insisted that he had heard of something truly frightening. To this day, I regret not pushing for the full story he was holding back . . . and now that he is dead, we have been piecing together all the things that he said off the cuff and reported officially. He often spoke in riddles and random ideas to ease his mind . . . but he could not tell anybody at the time, because we were dealing with four active 'moles' in our organisation. I'm sure you know all about them. I can assure you that they have all been accounted for and despatched accordingly," said 'C' decisively.

"Yes, we know all about that. It happens from time to time, just that you don't ever know when . . . or who it will be."

"The information I'm going to tell you now is absolutely credible and I believe it to be a serious threat to the entire world, should someone like Mudarov get hold of it. Somehow or other, he knows certain things in detail . . . and must wonder about the possibilities of using that information However, like us, he knows that the use of such information can change the course of history . . . if not end the world as we know it," said 'C' calmly.

"But what can be so dangerous . . . of such magnitude, that the entire world can be threatened. Our own intelligence has nothing about any major threat," replied a surprised Miller.

"It is all about a team of Bosnian mercenaries who gathered together many years ago to design and implant a series of bombs . . . nuclear, dirty bombs . . . placed into locations around the globe, to be detonated depending on whose side they chose to support . . . if their demands were not met."

"Nukes? Where are they . . . and where are these mercenaries? Are there any here in the States?"

"The good news is that the mercenaries are all dead. Every one of them killed when their plane crashed in the mountains over Eastern Poland, whilst they were escaping to Russia. We believe the Russians were responsible . . . getting rid of loose ends, and we think that Mudarov was also part of that group and knows what they were doing, but not the locations. The bombs are most likely to be secreted in public buildings, as far as we can tell . . . possibly in London, Paris, New York, Moscow, Beijing, Berlin . . . Hong Kong maybe. We just don't know where or how many."

"Well, can't we just look for them somehow? I mean they would have to leave a trace of radiation surely. Anyway, if all the mercenaries are dead, how can they detonate the bombs?" rushed Miller.

"Let's not get ahead of ourselves here. We first have to allow Ruby to find the information, with the location of the suspected bombs. Our top agent, Tian is progressing well in following her. We hope to consult with both of them in due course. We are tracking her in the Brisbane area at present," continued 'C' winking at Simon.

"Brisbane . . . really? replied Miller, unconvinced.

'C' knew that Miller could read his thoughts and continued with the details quickly.

"Then we can work out the careful dismantling of these bombs without the particular countries getting hostile, and to prevent repercussions from their agencies. They would probably blame us. The problem is that Mudarov is somehow using our networks to find her, so there is no point putting out an open order with ASIO or the Federal Police to find her. That is what I wanted to tell you.

I will keep you informed of developments and ask that you do not continue your search for Ruby, as it will only compromise our efforts to get the Davis papers. When we have a clear idea of what we are up against, we can work together to sort out the details and suppress any information external to our liaison.

Can I ask that you will trust us to keep our word and that you will hold back on Ruby for now," asked 'C' respectfully.

There was a mumbling and whispering going on in the background before Miller answered.

"You have our word. We will work together on this. Just make sure that if you go it alone without our permission, that we will act in our own interest to protect our assets, our people . . . and our policies."

"Agreed. Thank you for your cooperation and for your understanding," finished 'C' looking at Simon's reaction.

The session was over. Now there was no need for MI6 to keep asking their permission for any 'related' manoeuvres.

"They are not stupid. They will keep looking . . . and our man over there will keep us informed if they find her first. At least we all know what this is about," said 'C' to Simon.

"Oh . . . what do you want me to do about the other FIOs in Australia Sir? It must be rather uncomfortable all round with this sort of thing going on," asked Simon.

"Yes . . . Let's pull them all out immediately from that ridiculous 'meet and greet' fiasco in Brisbane or Pine Gap if they are there already, and get them sent down to Hobart. Tian has a good nose for making a hunch. Coltridge, Sikorski and five new recruits are in that group, including a friend of Ruby's from graduate school, Jenni Soames. We also have some people entrenched in the CSIRO and the Australian Antarctic Division. They may know something about the local boating scene."

Back at Langley, Miller was very concerned about the evolving situation. He had called the President. The orders were explicit.

"Max, get a new team together to find Ruby. They had four 'moles' exposed only a few years back. Do they have our confidence? I think not. We must not forget our own priorities to protect our country and interests. Get in touch with our nuclear scientists and the defence chiefs . . . but mind what you say . . . just the absolute basics to help us track down any of these dirty bombs," said Miller slowly.

"I'll get them sent up to Brisbane immediately Steve."

"No . . . she will not be there, I can assure you of that. Sure, they had to tell us the problem but in their usual devious British way, they have steered us away from the chase. She could be anywhere . . . so start with Melbourne, where she failed to arrive by train and caught the bus. When you find her, detain her and bring her back here. We will find out if those papers exist . . . without all the niceties and get them ourselves . . . and keep that butcher Mudarov in line. He must not let his fantasies get away with him and hurt Ruby. She must not be harmed by anyone Max . . . is that clear?"

Janet Paisley was staring at Ruby's photo on the 'big screen', wondering the same as Ruby . . . about how an innocent young English woman could attract so much trouble and lead such a complex life, full of intrigue and survival against all odds. Miller looked at her obsession with the image, and with a smile turned towards Max.

"The Brits may have it all wrong Max . . . it's the new-age woman we have to fear the most."

Kunanyi

Ruby had fallen asleep in her chair after watching only a few minutes of the film aboard the Spirit of Tasmania. She had not slept well for days. It was a quiet crossing as they headed for Devonport across Bass Strait, unusually quiet for what is widely known as a wild stretch of water. Several crewmembers competing in the Sydney to Hobart yacht race had died some years before in a wild storm that arose unexpectedly. The sea can be a dangerous companion when taken for granted.

The ferry, loaded up with vehicles and passengers arrived in Devonport at 6am, allowing passengers without cars to disembark within thirty minutes. Ruby was still travelling as Angelica Rossetti, keeping her sloppy beret perched over her forehead until she passed through the arrival gate. Then she headed over to the taxi rank.

During the crossing, she had looked over the paperwork that Davis had left her regarding her yacht, berthed within the Royale marina, a few kilometres from Hobart on the River Derwent. The boat was called 'Elaine'. She pondered on the name, wondering if it had any significance to Roger or if he had purchased it with that name. She reasoned that her Eric would have worked it out immediately based on his abstract randomised logic. Then it gelled with her . . . it was the name of Roger's lover, who had been presumed dead, but had been secreted away by Roger to safety in Greece to have his baby. He never saw her or the child again, for security reasons to protect them. Elaine had died shortly after Davis was murdered.

Their son Peter had grown up with a false name and had joined MI6 as a psychology profiler. He was killed in a hospital shoot-out by a high-ranking 'mole' when armed terrorists tried to kill Ruby.

Thinking about Peter, who had secretly followed her around to find out more about his father, she felt her mood changing to regret and despair again, and was now feeling awash with anxiety. She took some deep breaths and re-focussed on the job at hand . . . to get the boat keys and get some more sleep away from prying eyes.

The taxi driver took Ruby to the bus depot nearby. She was becoming very familiar with bus transport and felt quite relieved when told that the bus would be setting off for Hobart at 10am.

Armed with her usual oversupply of food and drink, she boarded the bus early and had a brief but pleasant talk with the driver.

"Yes, there's a big mountain next to Hobart called Mount Wellington or Kunanyi as the aboriginals have called it for centuries, long before white man arrived and started logging everything. The Kiwis call it a hill, but then they can't speak properly anyway. Some greedy buggers want to build a bloody cable car up there. Nah . . . can't see it happening myself. Not when the 'ferals' get a whiff of it," he joked.

She remembered that the last wishes of Davis mentioned that his ashes should be scattered from the top of Mount Wellington. It would have to wait until her next visit . . . if she survived the present one. The driver carried on his tourist awareness banter.

"My mate Davo has a boat down there at the Royale . . . not the new one . . . the old one across the bay. He reckons it's a safe place to stay when his missus plays up and kicks him out of the house for winning the footy. They barrack for different teams. Yeah, old Davo reckons it's a great little holdup. Tell you what love, I'll let you off at the highway, just a short walk from the marina. I reckon you want the one with the café and all that security and all. Is it your own boat or are you visiting?" continued the Driver, eyeing up her food supply.

"Just a friend of mine I met on my travels. I am Ruby err . . . Ruby Winters . . . do you want a bag of crisps? I have enough to last a week," raced Ruby, aware of the slipup.

"Crisps? Oh yeah, potato chips great. Oh and I'm Scooter by the way. Gary to the cops but Scooter to me mates. I had one when I was a kid and it just stuck, because I ended up crashing it into the local cop's car . . . it was all downhill and I couldn't bloody stop."

They both laughed, as more passengers arrived, and Ruby made her way to a seat near the front. Scooter got into his official driving mode, ready for the three-hour trip through the centre of Tasmania, stopping briefly at Campbell Town.

Sure enough, as he had promised, at an intersection on the highway near to Hobart, Scooter pulled over to let Ruby get out. A friendly man with his hand in the air tried to board the bus from the local pub on the corner, but Scooter put his foot down after closing the automatic door, leaving the man looking bewildered, as his football scarf fluttered from the doorway.

Ruby made her way up the hill and down to the marina's electronic controlled gate. She called into the café to ask for directions and bought a 'Chiko Roll' to try it out. Expecting a chicken taste, she asked what was in it.

"Mixed vegetables mainly love. It's an Aussie icon . . . prefer a burger myself," replied the worker in a 'hi-vis' shirt standing next to her.

"Where is the marina office? I have to pick up some keys."

"Just around the corner there," replied the woman behind the counter.

After presenting her identification as Angelica Rossetti, they gave her the boat keys and directions to where it was located. On each side of the gangway, small boats, sail boats, motor boats and boats needing a bit of care were tied up to the floating dock system.

"When the tide goes up and down, so do the gangways and boats," explained the marina manager.

There was a large yacht near the end of the long central gangway, which soon came into full view as the "Elaine". It had a tall mast and lots of electronic gadgetry attached to the mast and cabin roof. It was about forty foot in length. Alongside it was a motorboat called the 'Amazon'. Luckily the owner was on board, watching her closely like a detective. He had long unkempt hair and deep piercing eyes . . . definitely not a detective but Roger would have loved this character for a good nautical disguise.

Ruby was about to say hello, but paused to assess the delicate situation. The man first looked at her and then looked at the yacht, comparing and analysing some sort of predestined algorithm for working out who she was. He seemed to have some sort of mental condition. She knew that instinctively because of his rapid movements and darting eyes.

"Hello there, I'm Angelica, a friend of the owner . . . well, that's me now actually, on account that he unfortunately passed away some years ago, and he has left me the boat in his will."

The man looked horrified and turned away. Ruby continued to walk up to the yacht, looking for an easy way to get on board, glancing back to see what the man was doing. There were several fenders keeping the boat a good few feet away from the walkway, which proved to be a little bit of a problem for her.

Another person approached her from a yacht nearby, totally ignoring the other man and started rattling on without stopping.

"Hi there. Oh, don't worry about old Sid over there. He thinks he is the protector of 'Elaine'. Roger used to look after him and put up with his strange ideas about who he is. Thinks he is an ancient sage, no less. Don't quite know where he gets that idea from, but that's life I suppose. So . . . poor Roger has passed on has he? I'm sorry to hear that. I didn't see him that often but he seemed quite happy coming up here, and resting, as he would say. Beats me that a writer needs to have a rest, but hey, that's life I suppose. I don't want to pry about how he died . . . it can be most unsettling for the family. Anyway, this is my boat . . . 'Sun Spray'. 'Elaine' has been maintained by the people across the bay. Every year it gets an overhaul, antifouling and anodes . . . and sometimes a quick monthly visit, just to give the engine a run. Great boat and in the best of condition. A forty footer without the dinghy on the back. Oh, my name is Richard by the way."

Ruby was relieved that he had finally stopped talking.

"Hi, I'm Angelica and this is now my boat. I need to get inside, sort out my things and get some sleep. Nice to meet you . . . maybe we can have another nice chat later. I have been travelling for days and not up for anything other than resting. Now I sound like Roger don't I?" replied Ruby, looking as if she had limited time and needed to get on with things.

Ruby finally clambered onto the stern and matched the correct key to the door lock. She entered the enclosed control area and looked down the steps into what was a sizeable living space with seating, a table and a modern galley for preparing meals. Beyond that was an area with what looked like spacious sleeping quarters.

As she turned around to close the door, she felt someone standing behind her and moved defensibly to confront the person. It was old Sid, standing still, staring at her. He had caught her arm before it had connected with his head. He had tears in his eyes and looked so sad but appeared quite harmless.

"Dead? Did you say dead? How did it happen? Those bastard mole people he kept talking about must have got to poor Roger. There's always one or two who will tunnel their way through, for the right money, he would say. He was a cunning survivor was that Roger," he whispered.

Sid definitely knew more than he was letting on.

"Yes I'm sorry. It was three years ago in England. Did you know him well? I mean for him to tell you about the 'moles'. Errr, you do know that he wasn't talking about animals don't you?"

Sid looked at her and burst into wild laughter.

"Well they are animals of a sort aren't they? Digging around for information and passing on secrets. Yes . . . you really are as funny as he said."

His face again changed to sadness as he handed her a bunch of papers, pushing them into her hands as if trying to rid himself from the burden of keeping them safe.

"Here, these are now yours. He wanted you to have them . . . said you would know what to do with them . . . if he could never come back. I have waited here alone for many years. I was the one who told him about this place. My name's Sid . . . and you are the most wonderful Ruby Peters. We went fishing together and just talked about things . . . anything. It seems we all end up here to hide from ourselves. He talked a lot about you Ruby . . . and Eric. Is he with you? "

Ruby shook her head and diverted her gaze to have a quick look at the bundle of papers. There was also a sealed envelope, which contained what felt like a key. Sid looked at her distress . . . and knew she was not alone by choice.

"When did he give them to you Sid? How do you know that I am the right person to give them too? You don't know me except for the name. It is not like Roger to leave something as important as this to chance," she blurted.

"Yes . . . you are the one Ruby. I have been keeping a photo of you with the papers . . . see. It is you. He said you were like a spirit goddess . . . true to yourself . . . born of a longing for justice and equality. He only trusted you and me to handle his final requests. You and me . . . his only friends . . . and me being disposed to keeping a low profile . . . just to stay alive," whispered Sid sadly.

"You know my name . . . you have my photo and Roger's papers . . . but why did he give them to you Sid, instead of to the British Intelligence?"

Sid smiled through his damaged teeth. He looked more relaxed now that he was sure of her identity. He sat down and nodded.

"My name is James Sidney Tycroft, and I was once a part of Roger's team in Bosnia when we were both young and . . . completely naïve to the ways of field operations. We worked together before he escaped back to England as our operation became toxic. I jumped ship from the 'company' and headed straight to Tasmania . . . as far away as possible from the troubles in Europe. People take you as you are down here. The years have gone too quickly but being in exile has meant many difficulties, acting out as old Sid, the derelict delusional boatie in a far-off marina. The character acting was Roger's idea. He was always fooling around with his disguises and tricks, he was. And in exile I must remain . . . and it looks like you are now in the same boat . . . if you know what I mean."

Ruby looked at his deep-set eyes and furrowed brow as she allowed him to continue the story he had wanted to tell someone for a long time.

"Just get rid of that Angelica name . . . far too loud . . . and stick with a simple nickname . . . like Rose or Sal. It is a pity that you are so young, in a way, having to go into exile at your age. At least you are in a safe place as long as you avoid anything official or mess with the police, banks, doctors, work places or government agencies . . . I could go on. At least I have found that you don't need much money to live the simple life. My boat has solar and wind power and I go fishing every week. I keep busy writing books and playing my guitar, writing words to songs . . . but not singing. Now that would be a crime against humanity. I would get arrested for being an auditory nuisance."

Ruby was spellbound. It was like walking into another world of make-believe with smoke and mirror surroundings.

"How did you ever slip off their radar? Were you reported as missing in action? I was told that it could not be done . . . that they would always find you one day," asked Ruby.

"I used one of the bodies that was burnt in an explosion to hide my identity . . . same height, weight, shoe size . . . and they all bought it . . . way before DNA testing, but that's another story. I will catch up with you again when you have had time to look through those papers. If you need any help . . . just be wary of that Richard or Tricky Dicky as we call him. He could get us both into trouble and into the spotlight. Best to avoid him where possible . . . he is a nosy bugger, looking for something to gossip about. Just remember . . . that I am a known nutcase and have to act like one. It's a great way of keeping people away and keeping sane."

Sid looked at her closely, understanding the similar situations they both faced, hesitating to put away the other photo he had saved. He may have been in self-exile but he still managed to keep smart by acting as if he did not know much and gauging people's reactions.

Sid wanted to make sure it was Ruby by watching her reactions. He already knew that Davis had died in a gunfight and that a psychotic terrorist had butchered Eric. He felt a lump in his throat watching her, sitting quietly before him . . . a testament to survival against seemingly unsurmountable odds.

Suddenly, he jumped up, reached behind him and produced some more papers. Ruby was on her guard again.

"Now I'm certain of your sincerity, I need to swap out those papers I gave you for the real ones . . . unless you want to read the last few chapters of my short story on water rats."

Then he quickly climbed up the stairs to resume his convincing act of being a mentally deranged hermit, walking in a twisted fashion around the walkway, muttering something about a seagull with one leg. Richard was staring at him in a curious manner, shaking his head as usual.

With a quick finger in the air, Sid made his way along the gangway towards the café. Richard looked annoyed, disappearing below deck, before peering out from the gap between his curtains.

Ruby thought they were all quite mad, locking the external door as she made her way to the forward cabin where the double bed beckoned to her. It was getting dark when she awoke in a sweat, surrounded by the real Davis papers.

A photo of a smiling Eric, which had fallen out of the bundle of papers, was staring out at her, almost signalling for her to think as he did . . . which used to annoy her intensely.

After a few moments remembering the innocent days of school and that timid nerd with a fresh excited face who had always loved her, she smiled briefly at the photo before kissing it and putting it into her bag.

With no power connected and the battery switch not activated for internal power, Ruby found a flashlight on a shelf in the cabin. She still had plenty of food and drink in her carry bag to keep her going but she remembered that the café would be open early morning for a hot tasty breakfast. The café owner told her that she was lucky to be in Tasmania in summer, while it was warm.

She started to read the cryptic details woven throughout the 'Davis papers' which soon started to overwhelm her. She then lapsed into a deep sleep, which lasted through until daybreak.

Tian's contact in Tasmania, Julie Szabo, a scientist with the CSIRO had orders to check the new arrivals at the Spirit of Tasmania terminal in Devonport. She had arrived too late for the first lot of passengers who had disembarked at 6-30am. She had been up since 3am and the three-hour drive in the dark to Devonport was always going to be a struggle for her.

Realising she was late, Julie decided that breakfast was her first priority . . . missing the departure of the bus. She could hardly tell Tian that, calling in with her report that Ruby had not come off the ferry . . . before taking a nap in her car.

Tian arrived in Hobart by air at 10am and read Julie's disappointing message. She took a taxi to her hotel and during the afternoon started making discreet enquiries about boating and moorings around the area, narrowing down her search area to a few marinas, and some freestanding moorings in Sandy Bay. She even had some positive identification of Davis visiting chandlers and boat brokers in the past.

Later that evening, at the Grand Chancellor Hotel in the Hobart city centre next to the shipping docks, Tian watched the news on television, enjoying some local seafood with a local bottle of Cab Sav. However, far from relaxed, she was trying to put herself in Ruby's position . . . now all alone with her thoughts and concerns, in the place where Davis had chosen to escape his worries.

A call came through on her encrypted mobile device.

"How is it going Tian? . . . Any leads yet on where she might be?" asked 'C' nervously, "I have made plans for you to have some company . . . all the attendees from that 'friendly games' do up in Brisbane will be joining you. That includes Coltridge and Sikorski . . . apart from the three newbies. I'll get them to do some data-checking of boats and registrations."

Tian was not happy, as he had expected.

"Just keep them well away from me Sir. I don't want Ruby to see that a circus has come to town."

"Now, now, they will be extra eyes, that is all, and possibly a diversion for the Americans as they will eventually be sniffing around down there soon. I also expect Mudarov to send his female assassin to take out Ruby . . . bloody persistent bugger. We should have despatched him a few years back when we had the chance . . . pure malice and greed. At least he does not have the papers, so maybe we can flush out 'lady death' whilst she is trying to find Ruby. Oh . . . and between you, me and Simon . . . you can expect me to keep up with the latest goings on first hand, so that I can talk to Ruby in a better frame of mind."

"Talk . . . is that the new word for interrogation?" fired Tian.

"Keep calm Tian. We need Ruby now . . . and we will need her in the future. She has the makings of what I have seen in you for years. She has a rare talent and quality for this line of work."

"Ha . . . flattery Sir."

"Fact Tian. You are both too bloody good to lose. Take care . . . oh, and make sure your hotel bill is not itemising your dining bill. The accountants have been after me to save money . . . speaking of which . . . we still have to retrieve those bloody tracking devices from Perth Zoo."

"Yes Sir. I think the children's train and a troop of angry orange monkeys are the beneficiaries of Ruby's latest gifts."

"Well, the last lot in London ended up on a bloody poodle and inside some noisy machinery . . . drove the surveillance team quite mad. Remind me to take it out of her pay when we catch up with her."

"Or we just don't bother tracking her again . . . with respect Sir."

"Yes, quite."

"Oh and yes . . . I have narrowed down my search. Choosing Tasmania is not a good place for keeping secrets. Everyone knows everyone down here . . . or someone else that does."

At the Crown Casino in Melbourne, Mudarov had just received a phone call from his operative hidden within ASIO. Tian had been identified by the airport cameras, which showed her catching a flight to Hobart. He at once started to plan how to get Matylda into the action and maybe arrange some 'entertainment' at the same time.

"Hello room service . . . can you send up some more champagne . . . oh and I would like to tip that nice young lady who came up earlier . . . yes, the nice blonde lady with that friendly smile . . . Natalie? Yes fine, thank you so much."

There was a knock on the door. Natalie entered the room cautiously with a service trolley, leaving the door wide open. Behind the door, Matylda was waiting to gag her with a sedative.

"Yes Sergei, she does look something like me. Now when I change into her outfit . . . please do not violate her as you do me. I will leave from the utilities exit at the back of the hotel."

"Good, then I will have my car waiting to take you to the airport my dear. The jet is already making a flight plan to take you to Hobart. You will like it there. Remember not to touch Ruby . . . until we have the papers."

"Oh, you are so precious with that wretched, skinny girl Sergei. I will only prepare her for your arrival . . . and then turn her into pet food."

Sergei watched on as Matylda stripped and dragged Natalie into the bedroom. Shaking her head with dismay before opening the door, Matylda was ready to start a short shift as a room attendant.

Moving quickly from the lift towards the staff exit and utilities area, Matylda made sure that those on reception at ground level were witness to their room attendant leaving the building through the foyer. She had 'to be seen' . . . but not too closely.

Poets & Moets

The next morning was pretending to be warm and sunny, until the dreaded North Westerly wind descended on the marina with a vengeance, rattling the wiring against hollow masts, whistling in spurts and moans, and slamming the boats' fenders against the rising and falling jetties.

"Good morning. Did you sleep well? I noticed you didn't have the power connected last night," shouted Richard to a woozy Ruby, still stretching and yawning from a night on top of the bed.

"Good morning. Yes, . . . I slept alright I suppose in spite of that hard pillow and loud popping sound all night. What the hell was that? It sounds like a faulty bilge pump motor or maybe a short on a relay," replied Ruby.

As Richard was about to explain, a wiry figure in a black cape and eye-patch rose up from the 'Amazon' and a loud voice boomed out some middle-English phrases.

"Arrrrr, it be a fine day but with thee wind around thy ears me lads. So, tis the time to bog in to some bacon and googly eggs . . . for those with . . . small ears."

Richard was not impressed and left in a huff, going down below again. He was getting tired of Sid was always calling him 'wing-nut' and making other references to his protruding ears, using poetic license.

Sid called Ruby over with a whisper.

"Did you get to read the papers? What did he say in between all that rambling . . . and what were all those tables of figures?"

Ruby looked at him with a blank look as he waited excitedly for the latest developments, but she just sighed, sitting down on the side of his boat.

"I wish my Eric was here. He would know what Roger was getting at with his stupid cryptic puzzles and poems. Those figures do look to me like they could be some sort of map coordinates or passwords or . . ."

"A bit like those popping sounds you heard last night? You were thinking it was the electrics, but in fact, the noise you heard was made by hundreds of pistol shrimps. Nothing is, as it seems Ruby. Now there's a piece of advice from Roger himself," chimed in Sid.

"Pistol shrimps? What . . . like prawns or something?"

"Yeah, busy little critters with one small front claw and one massive one. They close their big claw so quick that it causes an air bubble to form and then implode in an instant. That causes it to emit light at five thousand degrees Centigrade as the sound wave kills its prey stone dead."

"Wow, who would have thought," exclaimed Ruby before thinking about his suggestion, "So you reckon I'm looking at the wording of these letters the wrong way Sid."

"Who knows . . . but it must be in a format that Roger would have created, so as only you and Eric . . . oh, yes I'm sorry to hear about your terrible loss, Ruby," he replied, averting his gaze.

Ruby smiled gently at his compassion before continuing.

"You're right Sid. I will have another look. Maybe we can go through each page together. Bounce ideas around according to how Roger would have generated such a pattern."

"Righto, just give me another hour, so that Richard clears off on his regular jaunt . . . well whatever he does for the rest of the day. Rumour has it that he was a police officer . . . bundled out of the force because of his bad temper and being a bloody nuisance they say. I can't say he fits into that mould though. He is too soft and is always complaining. Anyway . . . getting back, I reckon Roger uses a key word or idea to construct his train of thought. Have a look at the tables again and see if they match coordinates or serial numbers or represent specific words. I don't know."

Ruby made her way to the café and ordered the full English breakfast with a Chai Latte, sitting down outside on the combined wooden bench and table modules. The staff brought out the huge plate, complete with fried-bread and mushrooms.

Everyone passing by said hello or waved, especially the workers from the nearby boat-building company. They had never seen such a beauty who seemed like the 'everyday girl' but had that 'something special' about her that made her stand out. Ruby knew all too well, that when trying to blend into the background, such a reaction was rather a hindrance . . . although Ruby did like the look of some of them. Many were amazed at how she was tackling a huge breakfast with such gusto.

Around 10am, Ruby noticed Richard getting into his car, looking over at her and checking his watch. She was sure he shook his head in dismay again. A familiar trait was emerging in this fusty near neighbour.

She wandered down to the 'Elaine' and waited for Sid to join her, noticing that the 15 Amp, orange power-lead from her boat to the shore supply was now connected and turned on. There was also a box of provisions sitting on the back decking. She opened up the cabin door and stowed away the goods. Old Sid certainly had a good eye for tasty food. Looking around the galley, she found an electric jug and filled it. It worked perfectly.

Sid knocked lightly on the cabin roof and called her name quietly. The smell of fresh coffee had wafted by his boat.

> "Hey Ruby, how are you doing? Enjoy your big breakfast? I told you it was a great start for the day."

> "Come in Sid. Yes, I loved the breakfast . . . it reminds me of when I used to visit Eric at his parents hotel."

She stopped for a moment before looking at Sid, who was looking around the cabin in hesitation as to what he should say.

> "Don't worry Sid. I can cope with it better now, as we all must . . . it just takes a moment or two to get over looking back sometimes."

> "Aye I have the same thoughts some days lass . . . but they should never be forgotten . . . just placed in a safe place at the corner of your mind. Now then . . . where are those papers?"

Ruby was already arranging them in pages of texts and tables. On the first page was what looked like a poem, a riddle . . . or both.

'Six ways they sang to each other over time,

Then each one was a mother's hame

Waiting for sleepers to cease their voices

Then mothers once dormant would now be primed

Awaiting a master to invoke Goliath's revenge

Fungi clouded fire and wind

For You Are Two and thirty five released

Unless archaic places have removed their hearts'

"Crikey Sid. Well, I am just going to pick out a few areas where I think I know what he is suggesting . . . and then work out the whole of it later. That is what Eric told me he did. Just jot down random snippets of ideas and see what comes up. He always was a sort of cryptic fanatic."

"Just like Roger. It must be in their blood to want to complicate the simple and simplify the complex . . . now you've got me going in riddles."

They both laughed and stared at the page. Ruby went first.

"Right then, I can see a few things that stand out if given a wide meaning like Roger would use. Do not forget the context of all this . . . a threat or information about a major problem that he could not tell MI6 . . . or anybody at the time because it is so dangerous. Well I see 'hame' to mean home . . . and sleepers to mean sleeping agents . . . 'dormant now primed' sounds like a weapon or an uprising . . . and 'archaic place' is somewhere old or known for its history. That is it, I'm done. Now it's your turn Sid."

Sid was quiet, eyes screwed up and thinking out aloud.

"Sleepers . . . bomb . . . fungi cloud. Oh god no! He's talking about a nuclear bomb . . . maybe more than one," he said with a raised voice.

Ruby was reading his information into the remaining lines.

"For You Are Two and Thirty Five . . . Sid . . . Sid those capital letters for 'You Are' . . . he means . . ."

"UR 235 . . . Uranium!" they both said together.

"I can't understand the first part at all. Maybe we need to get hold of a scientist or electronics bod," said Ruby.

"No, I know what he is saying Ruby. We used to set off delayed bombs in our work overseas . . . having a bomb in one location with a frequency module and a frequency device in another location. The mode of action was that the two frequencies would combine at the site of the bomb, creating what we call a 'beat frequency'. All we had to do was to stop the frequency device at either location to prime the bomb and set its timer countdown. The beat frequency was used to stop anyone trying to defuse the bomb if they attempted to stop either of the primary frequencies."

"But where are they Sid? Is there one bomb and six frequency devices . . . or six bombs . . . all talking to each other? Roger must have been scared to release this information at a time when those 'moles' were still within the 'company'.

"That's what he kept on about all the time. Talking about the 'moles' and who they were. Now then, we have not answered the final line Ruby, where 'archaic places have removed their hearts'. I take that to mean the main explosives . . . yes definitely five or maybe six of them . . . are located in historical places . . . locations with historical significance . . . or museums. They would have to be somewhere that is not subject to change and disruption over time."

"And museums are most likely because they are usually inner-city and near places of government and business. It seems to be what Roger was saying," added Ruby.

"So now we should find some correlation between what we have worked out and those tables of figures. I am damn positive that he would have written the locations in code. It could be a long day."

"And who do we tell then Sid? Who can we trust to handle the finding and dismantling of these devices?"

"We need to work out where they are first Ruby. Exactly where they are and any other information about them . . . frequencies, types of bomb, detonators . . . and why they were put there in the first place," said Sid, still thinking of more ramifications of such a plan.

"And who put them there . . . and where are those people now. I wonder if those are the people who are following me, hoping that I will find this information for them to use."

"Did you get a look at them at all Ruby . . . or is there anything else you know about why they would know you had this information?"

Ruby thought back over that last few years and then her dealings with 'C' . . . at the graduation . . . the way he absorbed her into his own offices . . . with Tian, the surveillance, the promotion to Level 3 . . . it all seemed to fit.

"I've made a grave error Sid. I have excluded the 'company' and treated them as if they were all against me . . . and Roger. They knew all the time what I would find and I have been obstructive and hostile, blaming them for the way my life has turned out. They were not the enemy at all. I wish they had told me about all this."

Sid looked through the window, thinking about his own exile, and how he had contrived to lock himself away from reality and how the dark side of the world had affected his judgement. He looked back at Ruby with a look of regret in his eyes.

"We have both been such fools Ruby . . . more so me, for having turned my back on my country . . . my family . . ."

Ruby put her hand on his shoulder, feeling his pain as her own. She stood up slowly and took a deep breath.

"We have to get back into the action Sid. We were born to do this one thing . . . together. Together we are going to save our world from destruction and those who want nothing more than to ruin other people's lives . . . just for greed. I can get us back Sid . . . without going through the normal channels . . . that would be too risky. I have a very close friend who will know what to do . . . Harry . . . my long-suffering father. He will love me until the day he dies . . . no matter what I do. He will be able to sort out our return."

Sid was relieved at the prospect of leaving his home of many years, to leave a 'nothing life' of the living dead, back into a meaningful role as a protector of the realm.

Ruby started thinking about Jack, sitting next to her on the way to Perth from Heathrow. Ruby looked up at Sid.

"Do we really want to live forever Sid . . . or live a good life to the best of our abilities?"

Sid knew the answer to that but just nodded at her resolve.

"Some other things come to mind Sid. I don't know if you know Jacko, but one of his people in Perth, Pomphrey, thought that maybe the CIA killed Cathy and Jack . . . they were the two people who were sent to monitor me on my way to Australia."

"Ah yes, good old Jacko. He has had a rough ride for quite a while. We worked together with Roger in the Balkans. Out of business now of course. Lost a lot of his companions," interrupted Sid.

"But he died in those raids in Blackpool didn't he? That's another odd link to my travels and Roger's papers."

"No Ruby . . . Jacko survived the attack . . . but not his best mates . . . and poor old 'shifter' is now on his own in London. They will both be feeling the loss of their friends. You can't kill off old Jacko, not without a good fight."

"Jacko alive? . . . That's the best news I've had in a while."

"So getting back . . . I don't believe the CIA would kill your two friends or attack Jacko's offices in England and Perth. No, absolutely not, unless it was a rogue agent, but it sounds to me like some other organisation . . . and I mean globally organised, must be involved to do all that. They will be the the ones trying to find you for the information you have now found . . . and hopefully decoded. The question is who . . .

and what do they intend to do with that information. That almost answers itself . . . blackmail, extortion or malicious use of the weapons to create uncertainty in military responses," whispered Sid.

Sid caught a glimpse of Richard walking away from his boat, staring at the ground and looking very upset. With nothing more to hide, Sid left the boat and walked straight up to Richard. As he got closer, he could see that Richard was pulling a suitcase. He looked totally defeated as much as one can, with just the residual energy to leave for a quieter place.

"You off on holidays from your boating holiday mate," chirped in Sid without his usual acting up.

Richard looked so tired and frail as he put the case down, turning to Sid with a sigh. His back seemed more bent somehow.

"No Sid, I am going into hospital for an operation. If I do not see you again . . . well, I am sorry for being such a snoop. I did not mean any harm but I guess I have just become withdrawn a little too much lately. We both have something in common you know Sid . . . hiding from something so overwhelming, that it has consumed us . . . defeated our will to think ahead."

"How do you mean mate?"

'We all just come down here to die . . . retire, relax . . . avoid people and our problems . . . putting up with the cold weather as penance, only to hang around for the inevitable."

Sid looked at him with pity. Not just for Richard, but for both of them. It was becoming a day of facing reality on a grand scale. He put his hand firmly on Richard's back.

"We've both been a bit off over the years mate. I am not quite as daft as you think, you know . . . it was just my way of keeping to myself. Look . . . if there is anything you want doing while you are having your 'op' . . . just let me know. It is high time we both faced up to reality without the guards up. I'm sure you'll be just fine and if you want a lift to the hospital, give me a hoi," said Sid quietly with a smile, feeling his pain.

Richard just nodded and proceeded to go to shore, before turning around to his new 'friend'.

"I knew you were just acting the fool you know, old Sid my arse. It takes one to know one it seems. You would be surprised. Thank you for your offer too. Look after the girl mate . . . she must never become isolated like us old fools."

Ruby was looking on through her window at the changed attitude of Sid towards Richard. They had both taught her that time alone was a great leveller of the mind, a time to sort things out as long as it didn't run out first. For her though, it was a distraction not to dwell on, as she spread the tables of figures onto the galley table, talking sternly to her inner mentor.

"Right then Roger . . . let's see what sort of a muddle I'm going to make out of your crazy figures. I don't know why you presumed that I would be able to decipher your 'doodling', although you would not have expected that I would be coming here alone."

It was then she realised that she still had to make 'that' call. The call that was arranged between her and her Dad on her graduation day. Such a call, sent as a particular coded message, would indicate that she was well, physically and mentally, but that she had been forced to go to ground for an extensive period. There was the further understanding that the authorities may have reported to the family that she had died.

She knew it would worry Harry but that he would keep the situation to himself, until he had brought the matter to its conclusion. Harry would do anything to save his daughter and Ruby would do anything to see him again.

Finders Keepers

The problem with crowds is that they can hide people who look like the norm, but unusual people tend to become more obvious than when even in a small group.

Ruby stood out because of her beauty, her height and slender figure, and her ability to generate such a mesmerising presence that it was impossible to ignore her. Her trusted beret, hanging limp over her forehead, matched with a large jacket, was no answer to deceive the trained eye. People around her would often stare, even for a moment without realising.

A similar endowment was borne by Tian with her fine Oriental looks and charm, combined with lightning fast reactions to a hostile environment, sometimes looking too alert, edgy or detached from her surroundings.

Facial recognition software and a determined army of analysts had already picked up Tian arriving in Hobart. The CIA satellite reconnaissance had followed her to the hotel, alerting ground staff from Australian Intelligence and the Federal Police. They were quick to work out that she was investigating the boating scene.

However, the field agents were unaware of the gravity of the situation. Knowing that six cities of the world were in possible danger of destruction by nuclear devices, would have added more pressure to their work. Many were still not convinced if MI6 was being truthful.

> "That Tian woman is already in Hobart, looking around boats and their moorings. That means Ruby has to be in there somewhere. I'll keep you informed," said the Army Chief, standing in a quiet corner of the corridor, after his latest meeting with the CIA director, Steve Miller.

Mudarov smiled quietly to himself, pouring another drink and looking at his latest conquest . . . still sobbing quietly. He gave that look and a casual wave to his bodyguards. They reluctantly had another grisly job to do, to hide his atrocious destructive lifestyle.

He continued talking to the Major as if he were planning an evening out.

"Good, good . . . Have they told you yet if the five nukes are the real reason for searching for Ruby? I know for sure they exist. I was there at the start of the project . . . the only one to survive because of the explosion. A case of 'sliding doors' Major. The only thing I do not know is their locations. When I find out, we will talk again about our common objectives."

"They have not mentioned any bombs yet Sergei. The CIA is keeping a lid on all the details. They are not too keen on the Brits getting hold of that information first. They only say that Ruby is wanted for killing our agents and needs to be brought in for questioning."

"Ah . . . questioning . . . a word with a new meaning for the modern rulers of democracy. I have not forgotten our deal . . . you will be in charge of the entire operation. You will go down in history my friend . . . and we will rule the new world according to our new set of rules."

Sergei put the phone down. He wanted to think about how he was going to handle the army chief, having already assembled his own team of trained personnel, capable of operating the tricky task of being able to choose which bombs to set off. The order of detonation was going to be dependent on who pays up and which country he needed to frame. They were ready to get the process of retaliation into play. A new call came through.

"Ah Matylda, I was just thinking about you my dear. I have some more news on your 'skinny bitch' and her whereabouts. Oh, and by the way, Tian is staying at the Grand Chancellor on the wharf. They always seem to be always one-step ahead of us, which is one-step too many. I want you to get rid of her too. She is of no use to us and only a hindrance. That should return you to the gold standard that I expect from you. Results Matylda, that's what I want from you."

"Really Sergei, you ask too much from me at times. Now I have two people to deal with . . . and do not forget the two at the airports. I am out here wiping your dirty dishes while you . . . Well I imagine our blonde hotel attendant has been 'attended to'. You really are getting beyond yourself you know . . . and then ruler of the world. Really Sergei, is nothing out of bounds?"

Sergei was starting to tire of Matylda and her insolent talk. There were many others to replace her . . . younger, firmer, transient.

"Dispose of Tian tonight . . . and then bring Ruby to me. You will be rewarded for your loyalty and determination, but this will be your last chance to avoid failure."

Matylda listened to his cold words, knowing that she was finished. She had a lot of information about Sergei that the Americans and the Brits could use and he knew it.

She had to see to it that he was no longer a burden to women, to the world and to her. Maybe an accident on a busy street. She thought about what to do. Eliminating Tian and having access to Ruby would put her in a commanding position . . . and a very dangerous one. She could even ransom Ruby off to the highest bidder. There was no turning back now. She had done some terrible things herself, to which any of the parties would use to see her demise. The only way was forward. She left her room at the Wrest Point Hotel in Sandy Bay and took a taxi to the Grand Chancellor.

Sergei had already planned a full assault on where Ruby could be hiding, gathering his team together and organising their flight to Hobart . . . with orders for them to 'despatch' Matylda to the bottom of the river, once Ruby was found.

Meanwhile, Ruby was working out the figures left by a frightened Roger Davis, looking closely at the precise locations of significant buildings around the world on Google Earth.

She guessed that if one of the places matched up, then the rest would be obvious. She reasoned that in London, a nuclear bomb or most likely a 'dirty bomb' would be best located at some historical place or museum, close to the city for maximum damage and effect.

On one page of the figures, there was another poem. The other pages had no text at all. Applying Eric's way of thinking, the poem was likely to be the key to the way the figures were encrypted. She pulled out the photo of Eric and kissed it. Then she pointed the photo at the words on the page.

"Do your work Eric. I need your mind for a few minutes . . . even if I can no longer have you here with me. See Eric . . . a puzzle . . . just like the one you enjoyed when we were together. Work it Eric, for me . . . you are my eyes," she whispered, putting the photo away and staring at the lines:

'1215 it was accounted by a formal Jack

It is what no man is . . . in trust to a clef

When will it sound no more, but a Tom's reign above'

Sid saw Ruby's light still on and knocked on the roof quietly.

"Come in Sid, we have another riddle to solve . . . the most important part of the jigsaw . . . the location key."

She swivelled the light around to shine onto the three lines of text, which seemed to leap off the page. They both stared at the first line of the riddle.

"1215 . . . just after midday I suppose, maybe relating to a clock or an activity . . . or the afternoon? What do you have Ruby?"

"We are talking historical Sid. I am betting that it means the year 1215, the year 'Magna Carta' was signed. There is a prominent landmark near London," replied Ruby.

Immediately she raced ahead of herself and started making sense of the first parts.

"Accounted for by a formal Jack . . . King John . . . and it is what no man is."

"A bloody island," shouted Sid, "It is located on that island where it was signed. Come on . . . you are more up to date with historical dates from school."

"Runnymede Island . . . now run by the National Trust . . . and when it sounds no more . . . 'atoms rain' from above. Quick we must get the coordinates of some statue or memorial there. That London bomb may have been dormant for more than five years but it is still active."

"Blimey Ruby, you are some sort of GCHQ on wheels. I could never have decoded that without you. Let's see if there is a monument there first and get the official coordinates . . . Roger would have used the one from Wikipedia. From memory it is a fair way from London though . . . maybe twenty miles or so just off Windsor Road. Why put it there?"

They stared at each other before Ruby had an idea.

"Maybe because it is only the 'key coordinate' to locate all the other sites. It is small enough to be pinpoint accurate. I'll check it out using Google Earth on my phone."

Then she had another look at the verse.

"Look Sid . . . it says 'in trust to a clef'. Clef is French for key . . . I learnt that in music. So it really is the key, to the whole puzzle."

"So we possibly have one less bomb, but maybe still a frequency device located there that links to the others as a network," replied Sid.

"Here we go. Runnymede, Magna Carta, monument . . . and we have 51 degrees 26 minutes and 40.15 seconds North and then 0 degrees 33 minutes and 57.72 seconds West. Did you get that Sid?"

"Yes I have it . . . There is a sort of resemblance to how the figures are arranged. It looks like the numbers are reversed around . . . and U is in there . . . and the letter L. That has to be U for UP and L for LEFT . . . and on a Cartesian coordinate system that would mean North and West. Blimey, we have it Ruby. Now the big question is . . . where are they all located . . . and how have they changed over the last five years with ownership, fires, security, access . . . deterioration?"

"We are going to be very busy for a while Sid. Let's split them up and apply the calculated coordinates back into Google Earth."

Over the next hour, Ruby and Sid solved each set of coordinates and found their locations, occasionally gasping in surprise as to where the bombs were located, with so little regard to the devastation they would cause.

Finally, a list of five sites had emerged, along with the key-site at Runnymede and some other numbers that looked like frequencies:

London	Shakespeare's Globe Theatre
New York	City of NY Museum
Beijing	National Museum
Moscow	Pushkin Museum
Tel Aviv	Hagana Museum

They both stared at the list and their locations as Ruby waited for her father Harry to call her with news about how she could contact 'C' directly, without going through anyone else.

"So what physical size are we looking at for a dirty bomb and frequency device do you reckon?" asked Ruby.

"I've seen an Internet document on such devices and basically how to make one. The components are simple . . . but the hardest part is getting the Uranium or other nuclear material to act as the toxic dispersant. Even exploding two enriched Uranium lumps together would give you a sizeable atomic reaction and render a city off limits forever . . . in our lifetimes. So you're looking at a ten foot pipe of about two foot diameter and then a box for the electronics . . . so about the same size as two refrigerators I suppose."

They were interrupted by Ruby's phone, which indicated a message had arrived. She looked at the sender ID. It was from Harry. He had sent a brief two lines of code, indicating that Tian was in Hobart and she had 30 minutes to phone her. Ruby explained the situation to Sid.

"You can always rely on family Sid. Tian would have found me anyway within a day. She knows me very well and probably worked out what Roger was up to in his breaks. She's the one who has saved my life . . . oh about three times now . . . and looks likely to make it four."

Sid was worrying about his own precarious position, whether to 'come in' or stay in exile. He looked at his boat. It was a quick means of escape to one of the many bays around Tasmania . . . or maybe out to sea for a while . . . or forever. He always thought it was a safe haven, but he was always homesick and felt lost.

Ruby made the call, carefully, simply, not making out they knew each other. Such was the protocol for 'coming in'. A meeting was confirmed. In 30 minutes, they were to meet at the middle point of the Tasman Bridge on the South side.

There was no time to waste. Sid and Ruby headed for the marina car park where Sid parked his old car out of the gaze of the security cameras. Ruby noticed that he always covered his face going onto the paving from the gangway, looking as if he was wiping his face. On another occasion, he carried a bag on his shoulder for the same effect. He had developed a habit of avoiding the cameras that were now second nature. He was used to being an outsider . . . to life.

Tian had already made her way out from the Grand Chancellor foyer, eager to catch up with Ruby. She had to secure her from danger, take charge of the 'papers' and at a later time, to try to work out why Ruby had abandoned the 'company' and their previous close relationship.

As she was leaving the front entrance to walk the short distance to the bridge, a woman wearing a 'Yellow Cab' outfit arrived in a stolen cab. It was Matylda and she instantly recognised Tian from the photo she had memorised. Matylda could not believe her luck at not having to check the hotel register to work out Tian's room number.

Sergei had not told Matylda just how good Tian was as a field operations agent and had martial arts as well as extensive weapon training . . . and real combat experience. She also had strict discipline and advanced cognitive and automatic reaction skills. She was everything that Matylda was not.

As Matylda watched Tian walking away from her towards the Domain with the white Cenotaph and views of the bridge, she noticed a group of four men coming out of the hotel foyer. Turning her back to them, she was interested in the second man in the group . . . he looked familiar. She listened as they headed down the ramp to the first taxi on the rank. She followed them close enough to hear what they were saying to each other. They had been drinking and were talking quite loud.

"What was it Tony . . . the Wrest Point Hotel?"

"Yeah, down around the bay apparently. There's a casino there too."

"Great. We can spend up and have a few more drinks when we're done with her."

"And the remains Benny? What do we do with her after . . . the meeting?"

"Nothing mate, we just leave her where she is . . . unless the window opens . . . that would be an option. The locals can deal with the mess. We are on holidays mate."

Matylda pulled her cap further over her face and hunched up her jacket as she quickly turned around, to get another glimpse at Benny, laughing and joking about their unexpected break. Her heart started pounding and she felt faint. Sergei had sent his bodyguards to kill her. He had now disowned her, leaving her stateless and alone in a foreign country and he wanted her dead.

Not knowing where to turn, whether to keep following Tian or go into hiding, Matylda ran off towards the wharf area. She sat down on a bench seat to work out her limited options. On seeing a rubbish bin next to the parking meter station, she rummaged through her bag, tossing out all references to Sergei . . . airline tickets, credit cards and a photo he had given her. She spat on the photo and put it to one side. Then she removed the SIM card from her phone and broke it up, throwing all the bits into the bin, before quietly dropping the phone into the water.

In another purse that she always carried with her for emergencies, there was a new set of credit cards and a passport in the name of Linda Carter, a throwback to her childhood dreams of being 'Wonder Woman'. She had been syphoning off Sergei's money for a while, for just such an occasion and had accumulated quite a healthy bank balance.

Realising that many people would be looking for her in Hobart, she ran back to the taxi rank, choosing the first cab, a 'City Cab'.

"Given up with your mob love," asked the driver with a laugh.

"I have just arrived here from Melbourne . . . and no, I haven't given up just yet, I just don't like yellow. It clashes with my eyes. Take me to the airport please," she replied sadly.

The driver looked pleased with having obtained one of the better fares for his shift and made out 'wavy wings' sign to the driver behind, who promptly gave him a one-finger salute.

As Tian approached the familiar tall, willowy figure leaning over the railings of the Tasman Bridge, Ruby just stared at her, embarrassed, yet overcome with relief. She had tears in her eyes. Tian just nodded her head with a smile.

"You have led us all on a wild goose chase this time my dear. Why did you not call me? I told you last time, on your very first day after graduation, that we are not the bad people in this world Ruby. You are with friends who have a common interest in protecting the world. You have lost your way again . . . hopefully, at last, I feel that you know who you really are this time. Now tell me about those papers first . . . I need to know that you have them."

Ruby looked at her and took a deep breath, letting it out slowly.

"Here, you can take them. I have even worked out the coordinates for you. I am now at peace with myself and I promise it will never happen again. I have a lot to tell you. Roger had to keep this information secret . . . because like me, he could not trust anyone. But he was wrong. We were both wrong not to pass the information on to the 'company'. Those who are trying to kill me would destroy the world with what I have found out from his notes."

Tian looked at her, weighing up the situation.

"CS Lewis," she muttered.

"What?"

"We are what we believe we are . . . CS Lewis."

Tian smiled and pointed back towards the city.

"Right then, come on . . . we need to get out of here, fast. A hit squad was detected arriving by private jet with one of them, Benny Gordon matched up on the Interpol watch list. He is one of Sergei Mudarov's stooges. Not a nice man at all. They will not stop until they have that information. We are also up against the CIA and ASIO. They have decided to handle the situation themselves even after 'C' told them to back off. They always have their own agenda. Oh, and there's a 'mole' at the top in Langley, passing on information to Mudarov. GCHQ are working on it. He is a bad, bad man Ruby . . . ruthless and like a wild animal," continued Tian.

"So how are we going to escape from this island without being detected?" queried Ruby, shaking her head.

Tian was about to explain the basic plan that was in motion when she turned around instinctively to see a man approaching them, slowly, cautiously, with sunken eyes and a sad pitiful look. Tian reached for her gun, prepared to fire, when Ruby recognised him and pushed Tian's arm down.

"Stop, Tian. He is one of our own. I haven't told you that part yet."

"Quick Ruby, who is he? Tell me now, hurry up or I'll take him down."

"This is Sid, James Tycroft, one of Roger's old team. He has been in self-exile for years, watching over Roger's boat and his papers, not knowing what to do with them."

"Tycroft? I know that name. My god . . . that must be a good few years back now. Gees, you were supposedly blown up in Bosnia . . . is that correct? This is most unexpected . . . two agents 'coming in' from different eras . . . and in a most crucial stage of a major operation. The papers come first I'm afraid."

Sid looked at Tian and then Ruby.

"Look, just go on without me . . . and pass on that information to 'C' and the others. Tell him I had to get out Ruby . . . but I should have got help. So, do with me as you want. I am beyond caring anymore. It has been a long, rough ride and anything is preferable to playing old Sid, the idiot," said Sid softly.

Tian was unmoved, looking all around her. This tramp was an unknown and superfluous person and she had forged a lot of careful planning into retrieving Ruby and the information intact.

"Go now, immediately. Phone the British Consulate and ask for a 'company annual return'. Then wait for further instructions. You are not to follow us or I will shoot you without a second thought. If you are who you say you are, then you will know that you are compromising my mission. So leave now . . . and they will look after you, as long as you follow protocol. Now go!"

Rather than return along the same side of the bridge towards the city, Tian pointed Ruby in the opposite direction towards the Eastern Shore.

"Run Ruby. We will get back on track after I have my driver pick us up. It is not safe to go back that way."

Tian activated her communicator.

"K4956 . . . Two pax to Roadie . . . Pick up at opposite end of bridge . . . tracer on. We have been compromised."

"Wait, Tian. We have to go back. Sid knows the locations of the bombs too. We have to take him with us," shouted Ruby.

Tian thought quickly. It looked like she would have to shoot him after all.

"Yes, here . . . take this. Fire it immediately if you have to protect yourself. You must pass on your information. Do not even think of me . . . just make sure you make it back to England with those papers. Here, you are now the custodian."

At the other end of the bridge, Sid was walking slowly back towards the city to pick up his car wondering what he should do. As he opened the car door, two men rushed at him, restraining him, forcing him up against the door.

"All these years of hiding out and then a pretty young woman comes along and you drop your guard. James . . . or do we call you old Sid? A living, breathing corpse, alone on a boat."

"Who are you? I am just an old man who has nothing. What do you want?" demanded Sid, detecting American accents and fearing the worst.

"Oh I think you can guess. You Brits are always trying to hog the limelight. Well, I reckon you just might have some important information that we need to 'talk' about. We may not even need Ruby anymore."

Just then, Tian came upon them, gun raised, standing in front of Ruby to protect her. Without a second thought, the first man instinctively shoved Sid into the car as the second man took a shot at Tian, wounding her in the shoulder, causing her to fall backwards to the ground. Ruby raised her arm and fired two shots.

The first man fell instantly, thrown to the ground as the other man turned around to defend himself. He was also struggling, trying to keep Sid from getting hold of his gun. Turning quickly, the gun went off, hitting Sid in the leg. Unfortunately, Sid, fell forwards into the dashboard, taking another bullet to the head. Ruby approached cautiously, stunned by what she had seen.

The man swung around again in a panic, watching Ruby trip and fall down only a short distance away. He had a final chance to secure Ruby, having already taken out one of his captives, but was faced with disarming and possibly injuring her. He threw his gun into the car and ran at her. Two short bursts of gunfire followed but it was not Ruby, who had fired the fatal shots. Tian slumped back down to the ground, struggling to talk into her communicator to get help.

Within a minute, a black sedan had pulled up and a man and a woman ran out to help Tian into the back seat car. Ruby quickly went to check on Sid.

"Oh Sid, we'll help you. Just stay with us and . . ."

Sid was gone, blood pouring out of his nose and ears, his eyes glazing over. Ruby grabbed the papers, which had fallen to the ground, then froze with the reality of yet another tragic outcome connected with her meandering exploits. She imagined the hollow faces of Jack and Roger, and Davis . . . and Eric, staring out at her from Sid's destroyed face.

The woman raced over to Ruby and dragged her into the car, closing the door as it sped off towards the Southern Suburbs. The sound of police cars and an ambulance approached the bloody scene, coming the other way.

The black sedan stopped near a covered Sandy Bay jetty where dinghies are stored and used to get to hard-moored boats. A motorboat with more people on hand was waiting in the shadowy waters to take Tian and Ruby on-board. The crew had machine guns and were in black combat outfits.

As the sedan left the scene, the boat sped away down the river towards Bruny Island and into the open sea. Ruby checked on Tian who was unconscious and bleeding profusely, holding her hand and shaking uncontrollably. Ruby calmed herself down to comfort Tian, applying pressure above the wound, checking her over for any further injuries.

Within ten minutes, the boat had slowed down, in what appeared to be a wide, black bay, facing into the cold ocean waters. Ruby looked all around her through the darkness and moderate swell. The boat was getting tossed around by the wind and crashing waves, as the others calmly looked out to sea, flashing a light towards an unknown target.

Suddenly the waters began to bubble and swirl around them. It was a scene reminiscent to Ruby's adventure in the English Channel when three boats were after her and Eric. As the boat started rocking again, a dark form emerged, towering in front of them. The 'company' had arrived using one of Navy's latest submarines.

The woman who was tending to Tian's injuries smiled at Ruby.

"You are safe now Ruby and Tian is in good hands. There is a surgeon and a complete hospital section on the sub. We use them for these discreet missions. There's also someone who wants to catch up with you . . . and to apologise personally."

"Who is it? I have some very important information to pass on. It is vital that I speak with my 'company' contacts immediately," replied Ruby excitedly, "I have to tell someone what I know."

The woman was now busy stabilising Tian for the transfer to the submarine via a special swing hoist. When they all were down below in the warmth and safety of the sub, the motor boat turned around to head back to its home mooring near Kettering.

Ruby stayed with Tian as she made her way to the operating room, still holding her hand. Then she turned around, sensing that something was going on.

"Welcome home Ruby, and not before time young lady. We need to get Tian fixed up first. I hear she will be OK after a transfusion and gaining her strength back . . . just a shoulder injury, but she has lost a lot of blood."

Ruby could not contain herself, jabbering amid tears, releasing fragments of information in between bursts of offering regret for her decision to disappear.

'C' was relieved that Ruby was safe. It was like a home-coming for a wayward teenage daughter, who had worked through her demons.

"I'm so sorry for all the trouble I've caused Sir. At least now I can make it up to everyone . . . I have Roger's private papers . . . it's all about . . ." she blurted.

"Relax Ruby. We have known about those papers for some time. He most likely obtained the information about those bombs whilst in Bosnia . . . but he died before we could gain his confidence . . . what with all that trouble with defectors and everything. Now when you are ready, we need to talk shop . . . just me and you. Oh, and I promise you there will be no more surveillance on you . . . ever again. It was such a stupid mistake to have scared you off like that."

The Captain approached the two and whispered to 'C'.

"Rendezvous coming up in one hour Sir. The recovery plane is on its way to take you home."

"Want to go home Ruby?"

"Yes Sir, very much."

"Captain . . . do you have anything to drink on this boat of yours . . . worthy of a reunion. This day will never be forgotten . . . the day Ruby saved the world."

"Really Sir . . . that's a bit . . ."

"You really have Ruby. You may even get a promotion . . . once you have paid for all those tracking devices that you have given away. I mean orang-utans, Ruby . . . really, that was a bit of a dig. Well, let's just get a stiff drink for now while Tian gets sorted."

"She is the one who should get the rewards Sir. Without her I would have died many times over."

"Persistent bugger isn't she? She is already our number one, Ruby . . . and she's not having my bloody job . . . not for a while anyway."

The both laughed and made their way to the officer's mess. Ruby placed the papers on the table. Something fell onto the floor. She picked it up and found it to be a poem that Sid had written. She read it quietly before placing it on the table.

"Poor Sid or James . . . he was lost in the void," whispered Ruby.

'C' picked up the poem, glanced at it and proceeded to read it:

"Breathing on my window, looking for my soul,

With a rising feeling that life is taking its toll.

Until the ducks start nibbling and the pistol shrimps pop,

Around my boat where the windy waves slop.

And the seagulls cry out, not in pain but pure joy,

As the cormorant dives, and the water rat stays coy,

As the flathead plays at the bottom of the river,

And only humans seek shelter. See how they shiver.

But my home is my boat, or more correctly a yacht,

Not that animals care, how much or what you have got.

For when they see me, they gather around,

To see their friend, who once was lost . . . and now is found"

'C' looked over to Ruby and sighed, shaking his head.

"Maybe you can find a suitable title for it. Keep it with you, for if you ever need to remember the time when you were once lost . . . and we came many miles to save you."

It was midnight at the presidential suite inside the Crown Casino in Melbourne. Sergei was shouting angrily on the phone at his bodyguards after they had reported that Matylda was not in her room and there had been some shootings near the Tasman Bridge.

He had already endured an earful of abuse from the Army Chief at Langley, for losing two more of his personal field agents and then complicating the situation by linking him to the death of an MI6 agent.

Sergei's bodyguards were now taking the full brunt of his anger.

"Where is Matylda? Where is Ruby? What do I pay you all for . . . tell me? You have crossed me for the last time Benny. You are now cut off from me . . . forever, and if I come across your incompetent, ugly face again . . . you will see what I can do to people like you. It will be your last look at anything," he shouted, throwing the phone across the room.

There was a quiet knock at the door.

"Room service Mister Sergei."

"I didn't order room service. What do you want?" quizzed Sergei nervously reaching for his gun, "Stand in front of the viewer so that I can see you."

Sergei could see the face of the young man who had helped him find a young inebriated woman the previous day for a 'talk'. The attendant had another young woman standing next to him, or rather slouched against him. What he could not see was the person holding onto the man's legs with a gun pointing between his legs. Sergei was in such a temper that another 'interlude' immediately appealed to his animalistic nature.

He opened the door slightly to look around the corridor. However, the door opened up so violently that it threw him to the ground. The young woman slumped to the ground in a daze as the room attendant ran for his life.

Sergei was confronted with Matylda, standing over him with a large knife, staring at him . . . and his crotch.

"No Matylda, no please. You can have anything you want . . . money, anything but . . . No please, I beg you . . ."

Matylda picked up Sergei's gun, waving it around slowly, before shooting him in the left arm . . . and then the right arm.

"Now you can't even hold yourself old man," shouted Matylda as Sergei screamed in agonising pain.

As he lay there whimpering, she watched him suffer. She pointed the knife at his chest and cut deep through his shirt. He started writhing on the ground again, crying out for her to stop.

"We are the same, are we not . . . you and me Sergei. We despise love and feelings because we fear rejection. So we kill, maim, torture and hate . . . and it has to stop. It stops with you Sergei, for all the women you have defiled and destroyed by your vulgar actions. I cannot see you harm one more . . . and you will not."

She pointed the revolver at his heart, before moving her hand slowly, finishing him off by putting three quick shots into his head. The scene was spattered with his blood.

Matylda then calmly walked out of the room, past the young woman who was now alert and shaking, and into the lift. She pressed 'ground floor', looked at the gun containing the remaining bullet, spun the chamber around three times and pulled the trigger.

Chance is a fine thing. No one heard the shot that finished her off. As the door opened, her body was on display in public for the last time . . . but people looked on in horror, instead of in awe at her beauty.

At Langley, a similar showdown was underway. Two armed officers and the Director of the CIA, Steve Miller were standing at the door of the Army Chief. They knocked, waited for a few seconds, then gently pushed the unlocked door open, only to find the Major slumped over his desk . . . a note freshly written, next to a bottle of whisky . . . and an empty glass . . . and his spent service pistol.

Miller's second in command, Max Carter walked in on them. He had received the latest information from GCHQ in England. He felt sick after looking at the tragic outcome before regaining composure, enough to convey the information to Miller.

"The Brits have secured Ruby and they have the information Steve. They are looking through it now. What do you want me to do?"

Miller already knew what had happened but looked surprised. He now had his scapegoat in the form of the Army Chief for when Congress would inevitably call him to account.

"Thanks Max. Arrange a meeting for tomorrow with their 'C' . . . and find out who takes over from this bastard," said Miller briskly, looking at the body with disgust, "Apparently we have a nuclear bomb somewhere in New York . . . and I may be out of a job. What else can go wrong?"

Derek Fowler from the local newspaper in Hobart was gathering information about the tragic Tasman Bridge shootings, from his network of sources. It did not take the reporter long to discover that Sid's car was registered through the transport department to a person at the marina.

The police, relegated to traffic control by the Federal Police were keeping sightseers away as several ASIO personnel, seconded from the Hobart Airport, scoured the crime scene for clues.

The local ABC news team was also on the trail and had followed the industrious Derek in a rental car. Their instructions were to nosey around the marina, looking for friends of Sid, in order to build up a decent news story. They could all sense that a major international incident was unfolding, having already had the first whiff of American, British and ASIO involvement . . . and there was a rumour that three bodies had been secreted away at the hospital.

Diplomacy

A specialised VTOL jet was heading for the airforce base near London after picking up Ruby and 'C' from the submarine. Tian stayed behind on the sub, on advice from the surgeon. She required another blood transfusion and the surgery had made her dependant on medical supervision for a few days at least. 'C' was quite enjoying his return to 'active' service.

"British invention of course Ruby . . . just like all the others . . . trains, soccer, rugby, fish and chips . . ."

"Pardon Sir?"

"This VTOL caper, vertical take-off and landing aircraft. Now every bugger has one. Well, I suppose you should be getting some sleep as we head back. I want you to be present in all our meetings with the military, science bods and GCHQ people, just in case they want to ask you anything about the papers or poor old James. We have not even touched on him yet, for good reason. Of course, he would have retired these days you know, but back then . . . well you couldn't retire . . . or tell everyone you were just clearing off for a couple of years or anything like that," said 'C' to Ruby.

Ruby nodded. She was tired and finding it hard to concentrate. 'C' suddenly looked at her quizzically.

"Surprised you didn't kick the blighter,"

"What? Who Sir?"

"That bloody rogue American agent who came at you . . . better than wasting a bullet . . . price of lead these days," he replied jokingly as he saw her fall asleep.

It was 2pm when they got back to Vauxhall Cross and ushered into the Delta 5 security meeting room. There were about thirty people present, representing all the armed forces, Whitehall, various scientists from the required disciplines and . . . the Prime Minister.

A taskforce had been despatched to the Magna Carta memorial and had detected a radio wave coming from behind the front plaque. Another group was searching the Shakespeare Globe Theatre for signs of nuclear radiation and for a different frequency radio wave.

"Any news Dawkins, on those two sites? Is there a real threat or not?" asked 'C'.

The chief scientist from the military weapons section in Defence Intelligence thought for a moment before replying.

"We have checked out both sites and have found nuclear material at the Globe Theatre but not at the memorial. Both sites have indeed got a frequency generating device, operating via a suite of weather satellites, each one operating on a frequency which generates a beat frequency between two stations . . . that is a combined signal with pulsating amplitude."

"And what does all that guff mean? Is it safe? Can it be made to explode . . . or more precisely . . . can we defuse the bloody contraption?"

Dawkins looked across at the other scientists and bomb defusing team. He waited again . . . hesitating to give an answer.

"Yes or no, Dawkins? Hell man, I don't want to know how it works or what you have to do . . . but you must have an idea by now. You've been there all bloody day on double time," snapped 'C'.

"Well, I mean it has been sitting there for quite a few years Sir and the explosive charges are a bit weepy . . . so care needs to be taken there. Then there is the radiation danger from the two sources. They have what looks like liquid Thorium . . . not enriched Uranium, so it is what we term a 'dirty bomb' and not the generalised nuclear bomb pushing two chunks of Uranium together to get a critical mass. However, if this one goes off . . . you get clouds of extremely dangerous radiation floating across the city. As far as dismantling it . . . I expect your disposal people will know more than me about that . . . but I would think that the beat frequency generation is to protect it from tampering. Stop one of those frequencies and you set the bomb off."

"That is not what I wanted to hear Dawkins . . . but thank you for your graphic account of what could happen. Now then, can the bomb disposal crew get in there and do something?"

"We have checked all around it and scanned the electronics to work out what it does . . . more or less . . . and Benton here, our bomb expert, thinks that the device is actually . . . a dummy device . . . with all the trimmings to make it look like a dirty bomb."

Benton had joined the group and was looking very relaxed, eating a sausage roll with his cup of coffee, as if on a work's picnic.

"More or less? You think it is a dummy device? Well that is reassuring. Tell me Benton, how often have you dismantled an ordinary bomb . . . if there is such a thing . . . with such a cavalier approach and vague assurances?" asked 'C' looking at the flaky crumbs on the floor around Benton.

"Aye, well Sir . . . you see the thing is . . . all we need to do is to get the explosive activators away from the rest of the assembly. Then it is impossible for the main charge in the tube to go off, well almost . . . unless it is as unstable as the primary charge. Aye, I would have a go at it Sir. There are indeed similarities to other devices that I've defused."

"Yes, but were they packed with a radiation source that could poison half the population of London? Then there's the River Thames to consider and the downstream effect of leakage," replied 'C'.

"So what is your priority Sir? Defuse the bomb now or let it be, until it goes off in time due to instability . . . or the power fails . . . or the satellite falls from orbit. Or, we can at least contain it now, to direct any blast into a confined space. It's not so big that we can't enclose it in a thick enough dome of sand or hardened cement, with an open base," replied Benton.

'C' looked at the Prime Minister and back to Benton.

"Look, just do something man. There is no point putting it off until it explodes one day . . . in a week, a month, a year . .

. who knows and we are not prepared. That's my humble opinion," said the PM.

'C' looked around the room at all the frightened faces . . . all except Benton and his defusing team. Then he looked over at Ruby.

"I'm glad you found those papers Ruby and decoded the information . . . but we now have a most tricky situation at hand."

"Yes Sir. The thing is . . . I don't see that we can leave it for someone else to fix . . . or for it go off without warning. Someone has to take responsibility, so I don't see you have any bloody choice in the matter . . . with respect Sir," answered Ruby.

'C' raised his eyebrows as those nearby just stared at Ruby. The rest of the room was abuzz with nodding heads and low-level banter. No one else wanted to add to Ruby's advice for fear of devastating career consequences.

"Quite right Ruby. Benton . . . get stuck into it and defuse that bloody contraption. Take as long as you like but take all the necessary precautions. I would think that getting some blast protection to the site would be your first shot. Am I right?"

"Aye Sir. I will need about twenty trucks of bagged cement and sand. I will get onto supply and order what I need. Thank you for your trust in me and the lads Sir."

"If anyone can do this . . . you are the one Benton. You have our absolute trust. Get whatever you need and keep me up to date personally with your progress, and inform me immediately of any problems, that hopefully will not arise. Meeting dismissed."

The Prime Minister walked off with 'C' and Simon to a small office just off from the meeting room. 'C' knew what was coming.

"Look Reggie, your role as 'C' has come under a bit of discussion at Whitehall. You know . . . what with the 'Cigar Club', those damn diamonds, Ruby and Eric what's his name recruited by Davis at sixteen for heaven's sake . . . four bloody moles sitting under your nose. Well, I'm afraid I have some mixed news for you," said the PM slyly.

"You're kicking me out PM? It would not surprise me . . . letting me know in the middle of a bloody important operation. Things have not all gone well during my watch, that's for sure, although most things have been cleared up."

"Yes . . . cleared up is a matter of opinion. Take Davis for instance. He knew about this bomb business over three years ago . . . and yet here we are today . . ."

"May I point out that it was also during your time as PM too, but I can see your point that those at the top must take full responsibility . . . all of us PM. If Davis had been given more resources . . . well, that is now of no use to us at present."

"Now then Reggie . . . look, it's not all bad news. What if I can see our way clear to get you a knighthood, for services to the country and all that . . . providing this all goes well of course?"

"Well let's not lose our heads over this. We all hope . . . no we all expect it to go well PM. I will keep you fully informed of our progress. So . . . what are you going to do about the other countries involved? The Americans know there is a bomb in New York, but not the location. I told my counterpart that we were analysing the information and would get back to him."

"No rush there Reggie. Let them sweat it out a few more days. I hear Miller is set to appear before a Congressional hearing over their own problems with double agents and some financial deals that went wrong . . . diamonds, lost agents and that sort of thing. No, he won't survive that."

"Or get a knight hood PM."

"Most likely thirty years or more Reggie I would estimate, with clemency for finding out about the Davis papers."

"I wouldn't count on it PM. He obtained the information via a notorious crook named Mudarov who is now deceased . . . and was in league with his Army Chief who was selling secrets," chimed in Simon.

"Yes, it is a real a fine mess. We had better keep on our toes. How is Tian doing by the way?" asked 'C'.

"She is coming good, slowly. Excellent mental recovery and alertness . . . but I am afraid her days in the field are over. That shoulder will not hold up to the punishment expected of a top field officer," replied Simon.

"Too bad, she will not take to that too kindly. And what do we do with the now famous Ruby Peters, who's photo is plastered up on the walls of every security agency in the world? She is also a familiar name throughout Whitehall and has more bloody passports than I've had hot meals. She is certainly a bright one but does seem to lack the discipline to follow protocol. We cannot have a loose cannon in our field armoury Reggie. Do you agree with that summary Simon?" asked the PM slyly.

'C' was inclined to agree but looked detached from the argument.

"Yes, I do have to say that she has only survived her many incidents thanks to Tian looking after her from the sidelines, but she has a fine analytical mind and knows how to read people. I thought about putting her into GCHQ or perhaps into a training role. Her profile is far too exposed to be an efficient field agent after all this drama."

"Or maybe a suitable position in the Foreign Office Reggie? She is good with people. How about I appoint her to do something like that, still under your control of course . . . a dual position if you like, so we can keep an eye on her.

"And she can keep an eye on you. Yes PM, I like that. I'm sure that would be to her liking . . . just so long as she is solving problems. Oh and err . . . I would think that having saved the world by finding those papers and deciphering the content . . . that Ruby might be in the running for some sort of . . . formal recognition from the Crown."

They both laughed as 'C" poured out another round of whisky.

"I would also like her to go to those other countries with the foreign affairs minister and his team, for when they break the news about them having nuclear bombs in the heart of their cities. It would be good PR from us to have her mending the fences, especially with the Americans. Maybe she can explain the situation to them better than our crusty old Whitehall brigade. Getting her used to being with the diplomatic corps will be a mammoth task though . . . bloody liars, the lot of them."

Ever After

Twelve hours on from the meeting between 'C' and the PM, a make-shift dome, made up of hardened bags of cement and sand, surrounded the Globe Theatre bomb. It was strong enough to absorb at least the detonator blast and contain all the radiation. The next step was to attempt the tricky task of removing the detonator in order to dismantle the main explosive device and remove the surrounding radioactive fluids.

A new 'black box' had replaced all the frequencies that input into the main circuit board, mimicking the control signals from the other five sites. This prevented any loss of signal intensity, caused by the shielding effect of the hard dome. The time had come for Benton and his team to discuss their methodology . . . and who would be doing what.

> "Right, here we go then. Anyone not involved with this part of the process should leave the building . . . and the area. I want Freddy and Robbo in here with me, and a clear line out to the scientific team around the corner. I may need their help. Now, ready for a quick check Robbo? Radiation suits and visors on . . . computer system locked onto the motherboard . . . and my tools on the right hand side."
>
> "All set mate . . . you are good to go."
>
> "Thanks Robbo. Keep an ice cold beer ready for me, for when we finish up here."

As they laughed together, Benton was already sweating, fogging up his visor so much that it clouded his view. He immediately took it off and proceeded to patch in a code to hack the output algorithm, which controlled the operation of the signal to the priming device. His pulse rate was up to 90 and climbing.

Before he could let everyone know of his progress, a blue LED lit up on the motherboard and he heard a relay click, coming from inside the cylinder.

"Ok then . . . I don't like the sound of that, lads. Look . . . both of you, get out of here now. It only takes one person to remove the priming devices . . . and I can do that."

Freddy and Robbo had no cause to argue with him.

"Good luck mate. We know you can do this," squeaked Robbo with his heart pumping rapidly.

"Yeah mate. We'll get that beer organised . . . and thanks mate, you know," responded Freddy who felt sick to the stomach.

As they were leaving, they heard another relay click. It was closely followed by a changing pattern of red LEDs on the motherboard. Closing the heavy-block door behind them, they picked up speed and ran for the exit. Everyone at the operations centre was watching the two main screens, showing different angles of Benton, his test equipment and the unstable device.

Suddenly from the inside of the tube, a constant, shrill siren sounded from a piezo-speaker, for ten seconds, followed by what was obviously a countdown sequence of solid, loud beeps and more relay clicks. Benton looked at the equipment, not knowing what to do next. He realised that whatever he did was not going to make the situation any worse, so grabbing the wire cutters, he cut everything in sight, frantically, before throwing the wire cutters at the wall of the chamber and screaming loudly in frustration.

When he composed himself, he realised that the beeping had stopped. He felt relieved but unsure what was happening – if anything. The operations room buzz indicated that they too were unsure of the status of the operation. Benton just stared at the motherboard before checking if any wires were still intact. He reasoned quickly that without a connection, then there could be no further communication between the components.

After twenty long seconds, he was ready to call it a success . . . but then another relay opened and he could hear scratching sounds coming through the speaker . . . followed by . . . the national anthem of Bosnia.

Benton started crying, laughing shouting and then just sitting quietly while the anthem played through to the end. After a further five seconds, a smaller speaker inside the tube started up . . . with what seemed like Morse code . . . repeatedly.

"What is that guys? What does it mean? Who knows bloody Morse code these days?" asked Benton over the radio.

"Roger that Benton. We have our guys from GSHQ here. We are looking for some of our older colleagues. Give us a moment . . . no . . . get away! Are you there Benton?"

"Yes, still here. What is it then?"

"Are you ready . . . B . . . A . . . N . . ."

"G . . . you're bloody joking me. Who the hell were those jokers? All that work to make a silly 'Hello World' statement from a dummy bomb."

At the control centre, they did not know whether to rejoice or wait for an explosion as Benton got to work checking the inputs and outputs all over the device, laying open more panels and tossing them aside . . . they were all dead.

The device had deactivated itself and appeared to be fully disarmed.

"Where's my beer lads. I'm coming out. Yeah, I'm coming out . . . literally jumping out of my skin. I need a long holiday and then some. You bloody beauty . . . a dummy bomb to blackmail nations using bluff . . . and not the bang itself. Who would have thought that? That tube has nothing in it at all except some speakers and a solid-state recorder. That was what was making the relay clicks and had the music stored in it too. The radiation source is confined to just two small bottles of liquid, just enough to give it the authenticity of it being a nuclear device."

The operations room and the various centres on standby all erupted into shouting and cheering. It was time for them to rush out of their offices and head for the nearest pub. Ruby was waiting at her apartment, hoping for a call from the hospital to find out how Tian was coping with her wounded shoulder. It was time to pay her a visit. She looked at her communicator message informing her of the good news about the bomb.

Back at MI6, 'C' was with the PM, the defence chiefs and foreign affairs personnel, now happily scaling down their response crews and planning for the next step . . . the approach to use with the other countries involved . . . that is if they had the same dummy bomb scenario as in London.

"Think how many people have died trying to get this information . . . and all for the sake of a bloody toy bomb," said the PM in disgust.

"Far less than if it had been a real one PM. We could have had a humanitarian disaster on our hands, maybe even a full-scale retaliatory strike by the major powers," replied 'C'.

"I thought that Benton showed great courage in there today. This country owes him a great debt," said Simon egging on the PM with that sort of 'look'.

"He is not getting a bloody knighthood Simon. You have to draw the line somewhere," replied the PM sharply.

They all laughed and felt comfortable within themselves having 'handled' the situation in an appropriate manner. As they headed home to their families, with a different perspective on life, 'C' started thinking about the times he had worked with Roger Davis when he was a field operative himself . . . wondering what had gone wrong with their working relationship and their personal friendship.

In the end, it was only due to the unfailing dedication from the British Intelligence Services, that they had uncovered his secret . . . and then only because a naïve young woman had stolen his heart, if only briefly, from the atrocities of the dark side of his life.

Penultimate

The news about the disarming of the 'London Bomb' soon reached the ears of Steve Miller, nervously preparing for a frosty reception at a hastily formed Congressional hearing. He was looking for someone or something to blame for having to liaise with the likes of Mudarov.

Congress had started to look into his other dubious missions; the clandestine operations that he had ordered through rogue agents; raising cash from the sale of stolen diamonds; and the occasional 'hit' on whimsical notions of suspect, international dissidents. These were matters to be addressed at another time and place. National security was their foremost objective and bringing corrupt public officers to account –to face justice by 'the people'.

The conference line to England was open as 'C' wondered what Miller wanted so urgently.

"Miller here. Congratulations on finding that information from Davis and fixing up your own backyard first . . . keeping us in suspense about the whereabouts of our own nuclear device. I will not go into detail about my two agents who were gunned down during the process . . . by your agents . . . only because we think they may have been working in league with Mudarov and his band of revolutionaries. That will be my concern to deal with at the Congressional hearing tomorrow morning. As for your field agent Ruby by the way, she eluded us all. I think you will probably have some issues there yourself 'C' . . . but that is your problem. What I want to know is why you have refused to tell us where the New York device is located. This was supposed to be a joint operation. You set it up yourself in the first place."

'C' did not have to think for long.

"You were kept out of the loop because we knew your organisation has some . . . I don't know if the Americans have an alternative name for a 'mole' . . . but anyway, you put my agents at risk . . . and they were nearly wiped out there in

Hobart! I have had to sideline one of my best agents to a desk job after all that. She is recovering . . . but her days in the field are over."

"Are we still talking about Ruby? . . . I'm sorry to hear that."

"No . . . Ruby will still be out there, swinging and kicking until she gets what she is after . . . so beware of any future conflicts between us Miller. No, I was talking about Tian, our Chinese-British equivalent of an entire army . . .very handy to have around when your administration is trying to screw up the Chinese economy . . . and the Russians, Iranians, Venezuelans."

"No comment there 'C', I am CIA . . . not the administration or foreign policy watchdog. So, the famous Taipan lives on. We have heard many stories about her exploits and firepower. Yes, she will still be a powerful asset with all her experience . . . even from behind a desk," replied Miller.

"Well now, let's get down to the business about your device. It is sitting quite safe, in a quiet building in New York. I will be sending over our team of experts to help you disarm it . . . and I say that with tongue in cheek Miller, because ours turned out to be an elaborate hoax . . . plenty of high tech circuitry and bloody frightening activity from its motherboard to scare the pants of our Benton . . . and the PM. We spent days setting up a counter-active process to stop five frequency signals from making it go off, covering the whole lot with a hardened dome as well. It was a massive over-reaction in the end. I cannot guarantee that your bomb is equally as harmless though, as the Bosnians who set up this elaborate plan may have had a different attitude to American policies abroad . . . 'hands across the sea' not likely to be looked on favourably by that lot."

"And its location?"

"The City of New York Museum . . . but I warn you Miller . . . do not touch anything . . . until you meet with our team. It is booby-trapped by complex software. Benton will be the one to speak to about that. He will be bringing over some circuitry that he designed himself, to tune into the input frequencies, expected by that motherboard. It should be a positive if not hair-raising experience for everyone . . . oh, and I am sending Ruby and Tian over as well, at the request of your Congress. They asked to meet with her to get all this nasty business between us out of the way. My government backs Ruby 100 per cent by the way, with how she has handled herself. These misunderstandings have only arisen because of her reaction to being hounded by various people . . . including the CIA on more than one occasion."

Miller thought quickly about why Congress would want to speak with them, overshadowing his own planned defence of his actions.

"You can be sure we will look after them with the greatest of respect 'C'. I agree we must put all this behind us after we get New York sorted. By the way 'C', where are the others? Where are the other bombs located?"

"I can't give you the exact locations as I haven't set up the right communication channel with the other three countries. It is a very difficult topic for me to bring up over a cup of tea Miller, with our counterparts, but I can tell you the cities involved: Beijing, Moscow and Tel Aviv."

"Wow. They meant business alright, but . . . I thought there were six bombs."

"There are five bombs in total with the sixth location acting as an electronic key, to coordinate the whole show . . . and that was located near London, at the memorial to the signing of our Magna Carta. That is why we could go ahead and dismantle the device at the theatre. It was pure symbolism from a disgruntled bunch of nationalists. They were going to use the bomb threats to negotiate for better terms for their group. Apparently, we have nothing more to fear from them as they all died in an explosion somewhere over Poland . . . except for Mudarov who had stayed behind."

"And he has been murdered by one his own . . . a Matylda Fisher. We can prove beyond doubt she was responsible for the killing our Cathy Summers and your Jack Parton."

'C' looked at Simon standing next to him. It was still not clear if Matylda, through Mudarov had ultimately been under orders from Miller and his hand-picked mercenaries.

"There is another matter connected to Mudarov that we are investigating thoroughly . . . The attacks on a group of British ex-military, ex-intelligence individuals run by a person called Jacko. His bases in Blackpool in the UK and Perth in Australia were completely destroyed. Luckily, he survived and is able to give us an excellent account of what happened in Blackpool. GCHQ is looking through video footage of the attacks using facial recognition and we have two bodies from the attack party to match up. I hope they were not representing your people Miller. We would not . . . we could not . . . reconcile that, not on British soil."

"I assure you that we had nothing to do with any of that. I can guarantee it. I would be looking in your own backyard if I was you 'C'," snapped Miller, now thinking about his limited options.

'C' waited for the effect to take its course.

"I will let you know when our team is ready," he said slowly, before terminating the call.

Miller sat at his desk, looking at his accomplishments scattered around the room; military, public life . . . then at the portrait of his young family. He checked out the bottle of bourbon sitting next to an empty glass. His world was caving in around him and he could not see a way through. His secretary knocked lightly and entered gingerly.

"Sir, your wife called . . . she asked that you call her as soon as possible. She will be taking the children to Florida for a holiday and would like to see you about some financial matters."

Miller nodded with a half-smile.

"Thanks Jenny, I'll do that straight away."

He reached for the bourbon and poured out half a glass, closing his eyes, comprehending the effects of his wife's desire to file for divorce and take his children away from him. His service revolver was always in the top drawer of his desk. He checked it was there, staring at it for a few seconds before slamming the drawer closed. He stared out of the window wondering what to do. He stared at his drink but could not drink it. He had to get away . . . to think.

After a few moments, he grabbed his keys and went to the car park below, wondering if he should just get to his boat and head off somewhere, anywhere . . . but he knew there was nowhere far enough away, where he could escape what he had done.

As he travelled far along the highway and into the woodlands, his eyes welled up with tears, his hands gripped the steering wheel. Looking at the hills and trees flash by and the sunlight flickering between the branches, he suddenly swerved off the road, his foot firmly planted to the floor, hitting a section of steel barrier on a tight bend. The car jumped over the crumpled barrier and careered down the ravine, hitting rocks and trees before coming to rest in a ball of fire and thick black smoke.

The next day as the Congressional hearing was about to start, news arrived that Major Steve Miller, Director of the CIA would no longer be appearing and the hearing would progress without him.

It was unclear where he was and what he was doing. The official word from the CIA was that he had stepped down from office and required medical attention. The President issued a statement from the White House saying that he had officially placed a media blackout on any news associated with Miller's present whereabouts, as a matter of national security. Max Carter, as Millers deputy would now be required to sit in his place, throughout the hearing.

When Ruby and Tian arrived for their own meeting prior to the Congressional hearing, informing the committee that they had come with a team of experts to dismantle a bomb in New York City, the hearing was cancelled. Congress had been unaware of the situation.

It was obvious to 'C' that Miller would not have not passed on the information, until he had gained some sort of leverage from a positive outcome.

Tom Gregson from the New York Times had managed to collar Max Carter outside the meeting room, where many reporters were gathered, looking to salvage their front-page story from the postponed meeting.

"Mister Carter Sir, Mister Carter can you confirm that Major Miller has been killed in an automobile accident . . . Sir . . . we have unconfirmed reports from the state police that the body they recovered from the accident was that of Steve Miller?

"We have nothing to say at the moment. The President himself has censored all information regarding Miller. I am unable tell you anything more than what you already know . . . or think you know. This is an ongoing national security issue and we are dealing with it accordingly. Thank you," replied Carter sternly.

More questions were thrown at Carter as the media pushed and shoved, trying to get near to him. Photographers were clicking away at anything that moved. Their next major story was starting to develop before their eyes.

They also had no knowledge about the British bomb disposal team now busily working at the City of New York Museum. The area was evacuated and the surrounding streets blocked off with barriers and police. Some media were already tapping into the rumours and suggestions that terrorists were holed up inside, creating another frenzy, with media competing to get their story in before anyone else.

Heavy trucks laden with bags of sand and cement were seen coming and going from the site leading to speculation that the building was about to collapse.

The main media focus had now moved on from Miller, the CIA and anything else to do with his hearing. There were reports that a crew from England was helping with the shoring up of the site, leading experts to wonder what their own people were doing . . . and if the building was going to fall down.

Ruby and Tian were not at the museum however, as they were part of a separate mission trying to bridge the enormous rift that had developed between the USA and the UK. This new meeting convened at the United Nations building. Representatives from Congress, the President's office, military, the CIA and Foreign

Affairs all lined up to welcome their two guests, accompanied by a small party of Foriegn Affairs diplomats from the UK . . . some with more interesting backgrounds in the military.

The first person to speak was Donald Pearson, who did not state what department he was from, which caused a few raised eyebrows among the British.

> "Thank you all for coming along today. I would especially like to welcome our visitors from Great Britain who have come to address us, as allies and friends, to regain our trust in each other after some unfortunate misunderstandings, the likes of which we shall not allow, to happen again. Now . . . before we go on. To place all our cards on the table, I have now been given the unfortunate . . . or most untimely news, as depends on how you see it . . . that Major Steve Miller has been killed in an automobile accident."

There was a lot of talk on each side of the table with some nodding and others whispering their thoughts to shocked staff that stood around them.

> "If I can go on . . . please . . . I first want to pay my respects to Major Miller for his services to our country . . . and apologise for any actions or outcomes that may have resulted from our combined communications breakdown. We are investigating this matter further and will act on the advice we are given to rectify the situation."

The UK Foreign Minister nodded and mumbled in agreement, knowing about the covert criminal activities of Miller.

Tian was more outspoken in her sentiments.

> "We have lost many of our people by Miller's actions in the UK, Europe and Australia . . . and he should bloody well be made accountable for . . ."

The Foreign Minister intervened by grabbing her arm.

> "Thank you Tian for your observations, from a field officer's point of view . . . and we do take note of what you are saying . . . but this meeting is all about diplomacy and protecting our mutual alliance. There is no place at this point of time for blame and in-fighting. Certain things . . . happen from time

to time that is sometimes not worthy of reflection. Sometimes, things happen, because of what was so sure at the time . . . but was not well proven. Hindsight is indeed a fine thing when lives have been lost on both sides . . . as you well know and these lives should not be politicised through anger," he said briskly and without any emotion.

Ruby remained composed, now that her thoughts had been aired publicly, looking over to Tian who was still fuming. The Americans looked at them both, fully briefed on what they had been up to over the last three years. Some senators would have put them away for life for interfering in CIA operations, and bringing ill-repute for their methodology . . . the public . . . and their country.

As the diplomatic meeting drifted on, it was apparent to Ruby and Tian that their presence at the meeting was merely an admonition towards the British Government. It gave the Americans a chance to appease their public, with the perception that their intelligence services had done a wonderful job. Many of the smug American politicians quietly sneered and whispered to each other at every opportunity.

News of the New York bomb mechanism was coming through the communicators of the British delegation. The Americans had the same type of dummy bomb. This meant that there was no requirement to enclose the bomb in a hardened shell and the operation to defuse the equipment would only take an hour or so. It was time to tidy up some loose ends with diplomatic banter, finalise the meeting with a few chosen words that even Churchill would be proud of saying . . . and head home.

Another mind was mulling the same thoughts. At the Whitehouse, the President had received the same good news that the New York bomb had been defused and the sham meeting of cooperation between the Brits and the USA was toddling along to an acceptable outcome. It suited his planned media announcement.

The only sticking point was the expectation that when news eventually would break about the existence of the bomb and Major Miller's death, there would be an immediate investigation into the murky role of the CIA boss and his links to Mudarov.

The President informed his advisors at the meeting that all the Brits were to leave the USA immediately, even hinting at them making a 'show' of his personal feelings. They were to publicly shame the Brits for their role in Miller's downfall, if not the cause of it all, through their agent Roger Davis and his underage protégé, Ruby Peters.

An arrangement was agreed to that they should be driven to the airport by a fleet of Federal Police cars . . . with the media tipped off that they were being expelled for causing international incidents in London, Perth and Hobart.

The meeting finally came to an end with the last words going to the Americans.

> "This has proved to be a most opportune meeting of security and diplomatic personnel from our two sides. I hope we have learnt a lot from your visit . . . as you will from our reciprocal hospitality and understanding."

There was the usual half-hearted clapping with unsavoury comments made under-breath, followed by a mad rush to leave the area as quick as possible. However, four officials, sporting security badges and earpieces, held the British contingent to one side. Immediately, a procession of similar figures surrounded them and ushered them out of the room, rather roughly.

> "Look here. Be careful there . . . what do you think you are doing? We are British diplomats," shouted the Foreign Minister.

Tian was looking rather apprehensive at the goings on and approached Ruby from behind.

> "It looks like they are trying to frame us for a media performance. Make sure they do not hurt any of our group and I'll get onto 'C'. He expected some sort of bad reception . . . but not this heavy handed crap."

> "Now look, we all have diplomatic immunity in your country and demand some respect for our roles as foreign envoys," continued the Foreign Minister.

> "You are going to the airport. No stops. No talking. No nothing," snapped the senior officer.

A firm hand grabbed the Minister's shoulder. He was then marched out into the hallway along with the others. The security man was grinning as he shoved him harder, ahead of the others, causing the Minister to lose his balance and fall badly on his side.

He was not grinning for long. Ruby kicked him hard in the leg, quickly deflecting a swinging arm from another security man as Tian laughed to herself at ever trying to teach Ruby any sense of decorum.

The group was now in full public view and some media began taking photos of them and shouting out questions for them to answer. The guards immediately straightened up as they continued to guide the UK party into waiting cars . . . with flashing lights and surrounded by police cars.

Tian waited until last, to ensure everyone was safe before getting in the car.

"We are being tracked by the 'company' so no need to worry everyone," said Tian, "Oh and nice one Ruby . . . pity it wasn't aimed higher."

They arrived at the airport to a massive media frenzy all shouting and pointing accusingly at them. Rumours of them being ejected from the country as a reaction to the UKs involvement in 'undesirable' activities were getting prime airplay. They were linking secret information linked to Major Miller and the closure of the City of New York Museum.

"Is it true that the UK has been stealing information from within the CIA? What happened to Major Miller? Who killed him? Why have you been thrown out of the country? Who killed our agents in London and Hobart? What is happening at the museum? Is there a bomb?"

The security guards would not allow them to stop and answer the questions and pushed them along to a holding zone, near to where their plane was ready to take off. Whitehall and the PMs Office advised them to say nothing. Their experts were monitoring the new developments closely.

'C' was not that 'unhappy' about the current situation, which surprised Simon, who looked at the vivid news reports being flashed on the TV and then back at 'C' who just nodded, mumbling to himself with an occasional chuckle.

"Sir, what are we going to do about this media coverage? It has been broadcast all around the world that we have been thrown out. We are the laughing stock of the intelligence network for being so gullible as to want to take down the United States."

'C' looked at him nonchalantly and pointed to the bookshelf.

"It's all been done before Simon . . . all this nonsense and showmanship to deflect the truth. We want more of this to sink in with the viewers before hitting them with the truth . . . that we are the wronged party . . . and we can prove it beyond the shadow of a doubt. We defused their bloody bomb too, but did not tell them how we did it . . . and now we can approach the Chinese, Russians and Israelis to tell them that their cities have the same type of bomb . . . placed there by a terrorist group . . . friendly to the CIA."

"Yes of course, Mudarov and his crew . . . and he can't talk now . . . or Miller," agreed Simon.

"And the Australians will learn that his hired assassin, come personal . . . stress releaser . . . was responsible for murdering two people on their national carrier, Qantas. We have drawn in the audience Simon . . . and they will want to see a damn fine performance."

"You cunning fox . . . if I may say so Sir."

"We will look rather grand again, I'm sure of that Simon . . . better than before, I would say. Oh, I do hope the PM will see the irony of all this . . . especially after replacing me, in return for the Queen's sword at my neck."

They laughed and watched as their frequent sparring partner, the Foreign Minister fought back against the media and complacent security. Then the cameras panned in on one of the guards, limping to one side.

"Oh my lord . . . I think our Ruby has scored a hit there Simon," shouted 'C'.

"Bravo Miss Peters! We really must send her to more of these do's 'C'"

The Winner is . . .

One week later and the world was a changed place for some in the know . . . but for most people, just the same old, same old. New outrageous utterings from fools that threaten to destroy world peace are always going to sprout forth from those who would be better suited to medicated life in a mental asylum. Most times, things quieten down and are quickly forgotten. Sometimes nations must go to war to prove a point. In the case of British Intelligence Services, it was a time of reconciliation and unification . . . and a time to make good on their promises to be more transparent to the people.

The world media were reporting a far different story now, after the PM, flanked by 'C' and the chiefs of the armed services had called a press conference. They spoke in detail, about the path of betrayal and destruction that had beset the CIA, emanating from Major Steve Miller and his Army Chief, acting on behalf of Sergei Mudarov.

Roger Davis became the focal point of their story. They explained that his personal crusade to contain a rash of defections within the CIA and MI6, culminated in his protégé's efforts to continue often alone, with his work after he died in action, protecting the British people and their values.

The PM had publicly thanked their active agent who could not be identified for security reasons. He went on to say, that she had rooted out those people responsible and had uncovered a plot to blackmail the world, using nuclear bombs and assassinations. He pointed out several times that this agent was a young female graduate and that the people who worked with her would know the person he was talking about.

Ruby now had full recognition for her belief and admiration of Roger Davis, who a few months later, was posthumously awarded the country's second highest civilian award for bravery in the line of duty - the George Cross. The honour was announced at a private ceremony held to honour his accomplishments within MI6, with the formal medal ceremony taking place at Buckingham Castle between the Queen, Ruby, Tian and 'C'.

There was one more duty to perform.

"Tian, would you mind coming up to the podium please. We have a special thank you from your colleagues at MI6 . . . and from the people of your adopted country, represented tonight by the Prime Minister. For I have it on good authority, that if it was not for you and your dedication to your job, and to protecting your team . . . that Ruby and the Davis papers would never had made it back to England.

We would not have known about Roger Davis's last request to save us all from ourselves and all of us here tonight may well have been the recipients of not just the primary nuclear bombs . . . but also the resulting retaliation from fully automatic systems . . . poised to strike without any thought of their human consequences . . . should their country be seen to be under attack."

Tian walked up to the stage amid loud cheering and clapping, now able to display a little emotion and a few welling tears for the recognition she always craved for as a child.'

"Ruby . . . Master Tan . . . if you could please join us on stage if you will," directed the PM.

They both looked stunned as to what was going on, wondering what else they were going to say to Tian. Her father, Master Tan was looking very proud as he stood behind his daughter. Ruby was feeling very happy for Tian as the PM produced an envelope and a small box.

"Right now everyone, if you please. This is a most special day for me indeed. Tian, please take the wooden box and open it. It is a small token of our appreciation from all the British people."

Tian opened up the wooden box to reveal a medal . . . and no ordinary medal.

"But . . . this is the George Medal . . . how can I possibly have earned such a high honour as this," she said now holding back the tears.

"Now Tian, please take the envelope. It states your new position, now that you are transitioning from the field to a more . . . healthier environment. It is from the Home Office and from all those who have expressed the wish to see you continue your good work."

Tian passed her medal to Ruby and began opening the envelope. She scanned the contents quickly and paused to think about what she was going to say. She decided to read the letter aloud.

"You have shown extraordinary valour and dedication to keeping the people of Great Britain safe from danger by those who would dare to harm our nation, our people and our way of life. For this heroic service we want to thank you and in recognition of your actions, we extend an invitation for you to accept a senior position within the United Nations, the Peacekeeping Intelligence division."

There were gasps and cheers again as Tian declared that she would accept and honour the position. Ruby gave her a long hug before saying a few words.

"I am extremely honoured to have Tian as my friend and colleague today. It did not look like this day would ever eventuate . . . and not that long ago either. Tian has saved my life many times . . . not just physically, but also she has freed my mind and . . . well she saved me from myself when I was lost, when I doubted my work and my colleagues . . and when I thought that I could escape my conscience. I want you to know that I will never forget what you have done . . . for me and for the safety of our world. Congratulations on your reward and promotion. You are greatly loved by us all."

Tian smiled and nodded gently, holding back her emotions, as it was now Master Tan's turn to speak, as her father. He walked up to the microphone and stared at her for a while, wiping away a tear.

"Firstly, I want to congratulate my beautiful and honourable daughter Tian, on reaching this highest office and I am proud that she has served her new country well. We came here from China when she was only six years old and I always remember what she said to me once, when she came home from school after being in a fight . . . just for looking a little different. She said the other girl told her that she would be better off going home . . . and Tian said that she was home. So, I say to her that night, what kind of a family can bring up a daughter to be so racist at such a young age. And Tian then told me that the girl's parents ran a Chinese restaurant in the high street . . . and they did not want us to open another, in competition."

There were many laughs until Mister Tan looked out into the back of the audience, searching for his heart-felt words.

"So I say to you all here today. Do not fear for our future, but instead remove that which we fear for the present day. You can only do things, now. Planning for the future means working towards it in the present moment. Remember what has happened and imagine what could be . . . but work hard today . . . to keep people safe and our countries working together. Thank you."

Mister Tan walked off the stage with Ruby and Tian to a loud applause, leaving the PM to wrap things up.

"Ruby, do you still want to escape into isolation and think that you will feel free?" asked Master Tan quietly.

Ruby thought about old Sid and his arduous efforts to remain hidden from life. Then there was Roger who attempted the same thing and buried his deepest thoughts and encrypted information in fear. Something that should have been acted on at the time.'

"No Master Tan. I have learnt from Tian that it is not the thought of death that makes you fearful and tells you to run and hide . . . it is the fear of life that must be overcome . . . by living it to the full."

Master Tan nodded.

"But there is one more thing I have to do before going back to work . . . Tian . . . I have to return to Tasmania for a few days to sort out some things," said Ruby.

"What things. I do not think that the Aussies will let you back in on a holiday after what has just happened Ruby. What are you going to do?"

"I have to see how Richard is doing, to make sure he is ok . . . and see to that Sid's belongings are taken care of as he would have wanted . . . and the 'Elaine', the boat left to me by Roger. Then there is one final wish of Roger's to take care of."

"What final wish?"

"He wanted his ashes to be scattered from the top of Mount Wellington . . . to be blown away by the roaring forties wind, to roam forever and ever," replied Ruby.

"Yes, this is very important. We must respect his wishes Tian. This must be done soon. Mister Davis must have his last physical remains honoured by his natural world so that his spirit is set free," agreed Master Tan.

Tian smiled at her and her father.

"I have an idea . . . why don't we all go together and give him a good send-off. We each owe him our lives after all. So Ruby, how do you think you will get back into the country, without being harassed and probably thrown in prison?"

Ruby smiled with that wrinkled nose that indicated some devious plan was already at the back of her mind.

"Well I have this friend called 'Shifter' who is an illustrator of sorts and a master of copies. Oh, I think he could come up with a new set of documents for an 'Isla B. Bach'."

Tian looked at her and sighed with that resigned look on her face as Master Tan raised his hand to speak.

"I could go as Yuno Hoo Too," he said seriously before laughing out aloud.

They both looked at Tian who seemed not amused by the frivolity.

"I will travel on my own and meet you there."

They all laughed together at the prospect of invading Australia and Ruby was now at peace with true friends and an exciting future.

About the Author:

Stefan Nicholson, MA (Swinburne) has had multiple careers in Science and Technology, with a strong drive to author books and compose music. Born in England with a Polish father, the family migrated to Tasmania. Stefan then moved to Perth, returning to live in Hobart, Tasmania in 2013.

He is the author of fourteen books, which include novels, short stories, poetry and a book of comedy routines. He also invented an international symbol language called "Symbolic Art Notation" in Tasmania that can be learnt in a few hours and is suitable for language coding even at the kindergarten level.

He has also composed more than sixty musical compositions producing a DVD "Pictures of Life" recorded on seventeen tracks for full orchestra, piano and band.

He is a member of the Australian Society of Authors, a Fellow of the Institute of Scientific and Technical Communicators and a member of the Australian Society for Technical Communicators.

Stefan has spent the last eighteen years as a Technical Writer and Multi-Media designer on major mining, industrial infrastructure, and oil and gas projects around Australia.

He currently lives on his boat in a marina, near the city of Hobart in Tasmania.

A news bulletin on TV a week later, announced that 'C' was stepping down from his role as head of MI6 with his replacement still to be chosen. It went on to say that 'C', or Reginald Southern, would be knighted KBE in a private ceremony with the Queen.

The meeting with the Queen overwhelmed Ruby, as she was presented with a special gold brooch . . . and a letter of promotion from 'C', for her part in saving the world from a potential catastrophe.

The promotion was well away from further field intelligence operator duties due to her being too well known in intelligence circles, giving her combined intelligence work at GCHQ and also within the Foreign Office. Although it was good to be home near her family, Ruby had already approached Tian to see if she could be transferred to a more 'active' position.

Tian however, was feeling a little left out in all the celebrations. Now fit and well after further surgery on her shoulder, she had missed out on any official recognition for her part in the Davis saga, even though she had saved Ruby's life many times.

However, she fully understood that because she was a dual Chinese national and had in fact been a Chinese spy, recruited by Davis, then it would be probable that Whitehall may have a few issues with her 'status'.

She did receive an invitation to attend the official ceremony to mark the successful completion of the bomb-defusing project. She was also very happy with the outcome surrounding the Davis papers. They had been found and acted upon, and Ruby was alive and back from her lonely odyssey.

On the night of the ceremony, at a secure site just outside of Windsor, Tian was surprised that so many foreign dignitaries from the five involved countries were also present.

A history of the project, exaggerated by the PM for his own maximum exposure came at the end of the short service. Each country thanked everyone for the efforts of all those who had made the world safe again. Then they recounted their own version of events for the benefit of their own media.